CAPTAIN'S
CALL OF DUTY

BY
CINDY DEES

MILLS &
BOON

First published in Great Britain 2012
by Mills & Boon, an imprint of Harlequin (UK) Limited,
Eton House, 18-24 Paradise Road, Richmond, Surrey TW9 1SR

Special thanks and acknowledgement to Cindy Dees for her contribution to THE KELLEY LEGACY miniseries.

© Harlequin Books S.A. 2011

ISBN: 978 0 263 89584 1
ebook ISBN: 978 1 408 97755 2

46-1212

Harlequin (UK) policy is to use papers that are natural, renewable and recyclable products and made from wood grown in sustainable forests. The logging and manufacturing processes conform to the legal environmental regulations of the country of origin.

Printed and bound in Spain
by Blackprint CPI, Barcelona

Cindy Dees started flying airplanes while sitting in her dad's lap at the age of three and got a pilot's license before she got a driver's license. At age fifteen, she dropped out of high school and left the horse farm in Michigan where she grew up to attend the University of Michigan. After earning a degree in Russian and East European Studies, she joined the US Air Force and became the youngest female pilot in its history. She flew supersonic jets, VIP airlift and the C-5 Galaxy, the world's largest airplane. During her military career, she traveled to forty countries on five continents, was detained by the KGB and East German secret police, got shot at, flew in the first Gulf War and amassed a lifetime's worth of war stories.

Her hobbies include medieval re-enacting, professional Middle Eastern dancing and Japanese gardening.

This RITA® Award-winning author's first book was published in 2002 and since then she has published more than twenty-five bestselling and award-winning novels. She loves to hear from readers and can be contacted at www.cindydees.com.

This book is for my wonderful collaborators—
Marie, Beth, Gail, Carla, and Elle.
May the Muse continue to grace you all.

Chapter 1

"Next one of you boys who makes a comment about any of my girl parts," Alexandra Mendez declared, "I'm gonna have to hurt you. Bad." Sheesh. Wear one lousy skirt to the office—and not even a sexy one at that—and the guys went crazy. Pervs.

One of the several dozen soldiers clustered in the ready room passed behind her and flipped her brunette ponytail. "Hell, Mendez. I didn't even know you *had* girl parts."

The old hurt speared into her, sharp and bright. He didn't know. None of them knew how much she hated being "one of the guys." *Desperate choices...made young...to save her father...*

She scowled at no one in particular. "Anyone see Captain Kelley? I need to talk to him."

A predictable chorus of cat calls and rude remarks erupted. She was so *not* sleeping with Jim Kelley. But it didn't help the rumor mill that he hovered over her as though she was some kind of freaking moron every time anyone in the unit gave her a job to do. Which wasn't to say she wouldn't seriously consider sleeping with Jim if he offered. She'd had a massive crush on him for pretty much her whole life.

She rolled her eyes and announced to the room at large, "I swear, you'll never see it coming. A knife between the ribs, nice and quiet."

Laughter broke out. "You and what army?" someone called.

She shook her head and didn't rise to the bait. These Special Forces types thought they were such hot stuff. Nothing and nobody could touch them. Problem was, they were right about that most of the time. Just once, she'd like to give them a taste of their own medicine.

"Captain's in the colonel's office," someone finally relented and volunteered. "Secure fax came in a few minutes ago."

Ahh. A mission was coming down to the unit. No wonder everyone was hanging around trying to look busy. They were all here to wrangle a spot on whatever team was about to get sent out.

She clenched her jaw. She'd give her right arm *and* her firstborn child to be sent out in the field just once. Other tech-support types went out to back up the teams all the time. But not her. Never her. Maybe this time—

The colonel's office door opened and the atmosphere in the room went from jovial to supercharged in about a nano-second. Captain Jim Kelley stepped out. "Delta Company," he announced, "you're up."

Cheers—from Delta's guys—and groans from everyone else rose loudly. Over the din, Jim yelled, "Intel briefing in the conference room. Ten minutes."

Alex pushed through the mass of big, muscular bodies toward Jim. Ten minutes? Crud. She didn't have much time to make her case. "Captain Kelley!" she called. He made eye contact with her over the shoulders of the non-Delta company commanders as they groused at him and tried to get a piece of the action.

"Mendez, you got a report for me?" Jim barked.

"Yes, sir."

"My office. Now."

He was clearly using her as an excuse to escape the sleeve-tuggers, but she was okay with that. He'd be her captive audience until the ready room cleared out.

He paused in his doorway and gestured for her to precede him inside. As always, her heart stuttered when she had any excuse to get this close to Jim Kelley and his rugged good looks. He was a man's man…heck, he was a woman's kind of man, too. Those blue-on-blue eyes of his, the thick, dark hair cropped short, the strong features, direct stare—

Without warning, her shoe heel caught on the doorjamb and her right ankle rolled out from under her. She pitched forward and slammed face first into her boss's rock-solid chest.

"Hey, Mendez," someone laughed behind her, "you don't have to be that obvious about throwing yourself at the guy!" More laughter ensued.

Her cheeks flamed. Whoever said fair-skinned women were the only ones cursed with blushing when they were embarrassed had never met her. Her golden complexion turned beet-red with the best of them, thank you very much. Of course, she never really blushed except when she did something humiliating around Jim Kelley. And that happened a great deal more often than she liked to think about.

"Walk much?" he murmured, setting her back on her feet. "Maybe you should stick to flats, kid."

Face on fire, she glared in the general direction of his chin and mumbled, "Yeah, whatever." She was such a dork.

She couldn't even walk past the guy without falling all over herself.

"You need help getting to a chair?" he asked dryly.

She hoped that was a rhetorical question because she had no intention of answering him. She sat down on the cursed chair, and then remembered she was wearing a skirt. She should turn a little to angle her skirt away from him enough that she wasn't inviting him to look up it.

She swiveled in the seat, but, of course, the danged skirt didn't swivel with her. The stupid thing wrapped around her thighs so tightly she feared a seam would pop any second. She half rose to twist it back into place. But in trying to be subtle about it, she was a little too subtle and lost her balance. She fell back onto the chair, barely catching enough seat to stay in it and the thing rocked ominously to one side. She managed to right both herself and the chair, but not before Jim smirked openly at her from behind his desk.

"I swear, Al, I've never met anyone as clumsy as you in my whole life."

She almost stuck her tongue out at him, but they weren't kids any more. And besides, she was only a klutz around him.

The grin faded from his face and his stare went all manly again. "What's up, Mendez?"

It might be common usage to call people by their last names in the army, but coming from him, it made her feel… ugly. Nerves jangled like broken power lines in her stomach. She asked as lightly as she could muster, "Where's the team mission to this time?"

"Secretary of State's going to East Africa to discuss the piracy problem with various leaders over there. We're providing supplemental security."

That was a particularly dangerous corner of the world. Delta Company stood a more-than-fair chance of seeing combat on the job. She announced, "I want to go with them."

"So do I. But that doesn't mean either of us gets to do it."

"I'm serious. I've been attached to this unit for a full year and I haven't been out on a single field op."

"You've been on tons of ops," he retorted.

"Sitting in a van a hundred miles from the deployment and babysitting satellite feeds is not a *real* op. I want to be where the action is."

Jim's expression hardened. "Not happening. You're a rookie. You're a female. And your dad would kill me if I let anything happen to you."

She snapped, "Rookie techs go out in the field with the unit all the time. And you've sent a woman into a hot combat zone before—"

"Yeah, and look how that turned out." His gaze strayed to the wall of photographs of fallen heroes under a banner declaring them never to be forgotten.

"—and as for my dad, I'm an adult and this is my job. He can get over it."

"You're inexperienced. I can't risk my men's lives with you. When you've got more field experience, maybe we'll talk about it."

He'd set up a neat catch-22 and snagged her squarely in its logic. She demanded, "And how, exactly, am I supposed to get more field experience if you won't ever put me out there?"

Exasperation poured off the guy, but she, frankly, didn't care. She was pretty darned exasperated herself.

"Do you have a report from Chandler's office for me or not?" Jim asked implacably. He obviously thought the discussion about sending her to Africa was over.

"I'll go over your head," she threatened. "I can claim discrimination, you know."

He leaned forward, palms pressed flat on his desk, and glared at her. "As long as you're attached to this unit, you work for me. My decision. My call. I say you stay right where you are. It took my superiors a year to get someone into Senator Chandler's office. And I'm not about to pull you out."

Frustration and hurt warred for supremacy in her gut. She was really, really good at her job. Nobody was better with high-tech gadgetry than she was. She'd earned a chance to do her job for real in combat. He was just being pig-headed and chauvinistic. "If you don't think I'm good enough at my job to let me do it, then why don't you let me go back to my own battalion where my work will be appreciated?"

He momentarily looked stricken, but then he snarled, "If you do something intentional to make me fire you, you won't be getting any jobs in tech ops again any time soon. I'll see to it."

She jumped to her feet and miraculously managed to get vertical without mishap. "How dare you threaten me!"

His jaw muscles worked angrily. "You threatened me first, Mendez, and I don't take kindly to that." His gaze speared into her coldly. "You have your orders. I expect you to stay put in Chandler's office and keep watching for anything out of the ordinary. You're going nowhere until you get the dirt on the guy. Is that understood?"

She was so furious she didn't trust herself to speak aloud. She nodded stiffly before pivoting and marching to the door. At least she hoped it looked like marching. Disconcertingly, in the narrow skirt and heels, it felt more like mincing than marching. She gave his door a satisfyingly loud slam on the way out, though. *Jerk.*

He wanted the dirt on Chet Chandler, did he? Oh, she'd give him dirt. In fact, she knew just how to get it. She glanced at her watch. Almost five o'clock. Senator Chandler had a dinner meeting tonight with some caucus group. And whenever he left the office, the rest of the staff usually checked out pretty soon thereafter. She'd give it a couple of hours and then she'd move in for the kill.

Her idea was risky. Arguably stupid. If she got caught she'd be fired from Chandler's staff for sure, and then Jim would be *really* mad at her. Tough. She was going to hack into Chet Chandler's personal computer. And then in a few days, before next week's no-notice system sweep by the FBI, she'd unhack the senator's computer.

It had cost her hundreds of dollars' worth of beers and countless hours of deadly, dull baseball talk with her "buddy" from the FBI cyber-crime unit to find out when the next sweep of the Congressional offices was scheduled. But it would all be worth it if she could show Jim Kelley just how good she really was at her job.

If he wouldn't send her out on a real mission to get experience, she'd just create one for herself. Passive surveillance on one Senator Chet Chandler had just shifted into active pursuit mode.

Jim Kelley woke from a dead sleep to the sound of someone pounding on the front door of his stylish Georgetown town house. What time was it anyway? He lifted his head to look blearily at the alarm clock. Two in the morning? He swore under his breath as he rolled out of bed and pulled on sweat pants.

"I'm coming!" he yelled irritably at whoever was trying to bust down his door. He looked through the peephole and spied the distorted figure of a woman. A familiar one he emphatically didn't want to see right now.

He threw the door open. "C'mon, Mendez. Do we have to get into this again? I said I'm not sending you to Africa. Get over it."

"May I come in?" she ground out between clenched teeth.

"Are you drunk?"

"No!"

"Are you going to throw another tantrum at me?"

"God, that's a sexist remark. Let me in. I got something on Chandler."

Surprised, he stepped back. She brushed by him and he sucked in a sharp breath. She was wearing yoga pants and a muscle shirt that hugged her body quite informatively. It turned out that beneath the military uniforms and dull suits she normally wore, the girl had curves. And beneath the curves she was lean and fit. Who'd have guessed?

She glanced up at him sidelong and déjà vu slammed into him. Arturo used to look at him just like that. Same eyes. Same wry humor. It had been ten years since her older brother, his best friend, had died. Sometimes Alex was so much like Arturo it was spooky. And sometimes it was as though the accident had happened yesterday, the pain and guilt and loss as new and raw as ever.

"Nice place," Alex blurted.

"Thanks." Those stretchy pants cupped her derriere just right, and her T-shirt left bare a sexy little strip of golden flesh across her belly. Make that a flat, firm belly. And make that an intensely weird sensation to be noticing it.

"Must be nice not to have to live on army pay in this town."

Couldn't resist taking a pot shot at him, could she? Must still be pissed about this afternoon. He glanced around the chic living room and shrugged. It wasn't his fault his mother was an heiress, or that he'd parlayed the trust fund he'd gotten when he turned eighteen into millions more by investing it wisely.

"It's two in the morning, Mendez," he said, hinting not so subtly for her to get to the point of this little visit.

She glared. "I'm well aware of that. I've been working all night while you caught up on your beauty sleep."

Vague surprise registered. What work would keep her up so late? She was a junior flunky—little more than an errand girl—in Chandler's office. Surely the guy didn't give her work to do that kept her up this late at night. "Congratulations. You win the workaholic award," he declared. "So what do you want?"

"Get dressed," she ordered tersely. "There's something I need to show you."

His eyebrows shot up. Since when was she the one giving orders? He was the unit operations officer. She was the lowly support tech. Not to mention, why was she so tense? She'd come to his unit with a reputation for being cool as a cucumber under pressure. That and the girl was a wizard with anything that had wires. She would give James Bond's tech support guy, Q, a run for his British money. Something must be up. Something big.

Frowning, he stood up. "I'll be right back."

"Wear something preppy!" she called after him.

Preppy? What the heck? Off-duty his tastes tended to jeans and cowboy boots. But he was curious enough to dig out a pair of tailored khaki slacks and a dark-green polo shirt. He rooted around in the back of his closet and found a pair of deck shoes, too. He occasionally sailed with friends in Annapolis, and the shoes actually were handy on a boat. In keeping with the preppy thing, he skipped socks and slipped his bare feet into the shoes.

When he came back to the living room, she was perched on the edge of his pearl-gray leather sofa warily eyeing his coffee table and the foot-tall crystal sculpture of a seagull in flight on it. The piece was one of a kind, but he restrained an urge to slide it out of her reach. He snorted at himself. Apparently, it was an ingrained habit not to insult a pretty woman at this time of night.

"What's going on, Mendez?"

Her dark eyes flashed with something unnamed. He might

call it fear if it wasn't Mendez he was looking at. She didn't have a fearful bone in her entire body.

She answered, "I found something on Senator Chandler's computer. I could've brought you a copy of the file, but you wouldn't have believed me if I did. I need you to see it for yourself on his computer, as big as life."

If he hadn't known her pretty much his whole life, he'd say she'd lost her marbles. But Alex never had been prone to hysteria and didn't look as though she was about to start now. She looked…scared.

They stepped out into the sleeping Georgetown street. He glanced around for her piece-of-crap Buick and didn't spot it. "Where'd you park?" he murmured.

"I took the subway."

"The Beast on the fritz?"

She snorted at the idea that any car of hers wouldn't be in perfect working order. Good point. Her old man was the finest mechanic on the planet, and she wasn't far behind the guy in what she knew about cars.

"I'll drive," he announced. Not only did he prefer his zippy little BMW on the Washington streets, but he wanted fast access to the Luger 9 mm semi-automatic pistol in the glove compartment.

Traffic was nonexistent at this hour and they were downtown in a matter of minutes. Shocking. It could take Jim an hour or more to make that drive during rush hour. He even found a parking spot less than a block from the Dirksen Building, where Chandler's office was.

"How are we planning to get in?" he asked.

"We're walking in the front door. I told the guard when I left to come get you that I'd be back with someone to help me in a little while. He's expecting you and will sign you in as a visitor," she answered disdainfully.

"No spooky ops for you, huh?"

"Hey. If you want to break in, I can take you around back and rewire the service entrance. But it'll take an hour and then we'll have to dodge the roaming guards who, contrary to what you see on TV, are very good at their jobs."

He shrugged. "Why make it hard if we can take the path of least resistance?"

"Like I was saying. The front door."

Touchy, touchy. He couldn't remember the last time he'd seen her this tense. His curiosity grew even more. What had she found to make her this tight?

"Good evening, Miss Mendez," a night guard at the front desk said. "I see you convinced your colleague to come in and help you."

She sighed. "Senator Chandler's freaking out over some testimony his committee's hearing tomorrow. He made me dig up a Subject Matter Expert and drag the poor man down here to help me develop a list of questions. This is Captain Kelley, by the way."

The guard was thorough…and slow. But eventually, the badge with a big red V on it was handed over. Jim clipped it to his collar.

Playing his part, Jim said, "All right, Miss Mendez. Let's get to work. We don't have long if this hearing starts at nine."

She nodded and led him through the metal detectors to an elevator bank. They stepped inside and the door closed behind them. She stared fixedly at the doors as if she was uncomfortable being in a confined space with him.

"What's going on, Al? I can't remember the last time I saw you so wired."

The door opened. "Come on. I'll show you."

She followed him down a long hallway to a walnut door with a brass panel on it announcing this to be the office of Chester V. Chandler, the junior senator from Nebraska. She swiped her badge and then keyed a number on the pad below the card reader. A green light beeped and she pushed open the door.

They stepped into a darkened room. She reached past him to turn on the lights. With a quick gasp to announce it, she managed to get her feet tangled up and he had to grab her fast to keep her from falling over. Typical Mendez. He bit back a grin at the sight of her cheeks reddening.

"Lock that door behind you," she mumbled.

He did so and turned around. Alex had already disappeared into the next room. He followed her in time to see her sit down behind a big mahogany desk and open a laptop computer sitting on it. Interested to see what had her so freaked out, he moved around behind her to look over her shoulder.

It booted up and she rapidly typed in a long password comprised of random letters and numbers.

"Impressive," he commented. "How long did it take you to hack that?"

"Chet gave me the password months ago."

"Seriously?" That surprised him. If the guy had secrets to keep, why would he hand out his password to some junior aide?

"Whenever he has computer problems, I'm his go-to girl." She added dryly, "Turns out I have a bit of a knack with electronics."

"You're kidding," he retorted, matching her sarcasm. By the time she'd hit her teens, it had been clear she'd inherited her dad's gift for gadgets. He'd never seen a mechanical device of any kind that could best either one of them. Of course, the army had spent years further training her natural talent until she was downright frightening.

"Here it is," she announced as she clicked on a file icon. As it loaded, she stood up. "Sit down and take a look at this."

He replaced her in the leather desk chair. An email message popped up on the screen.

The package has been taken. ETA final destination 6:00 a.m. local. Will report when contents have been secured and delivery confirmation sent.

"Mendez, have you lost it? Why do I care about some damned package?"

"Look at the date of the message," she replied.

"The twentieth of August. Big deal."

"Wasn't that the day your sister was kidnapped?"

"Yeah. So?"

"Check out this note." She leaned over his shoulder to click on another email stored in the same file, and he was startled to register that she smelled good. Like fresh-cut hay, sweet and warm.

Another note popped up.

Delivery confirmation received. Recipient has not responded, however. Request further instructions.

And then a third note.

We need you to lean on HK. Make him understand what will happen if he doesn't play ball.

Disquiet started to rumble in Jim's gut. His father, Hank Kelley, had initially kept Lana's kidnapping secret from the rest of the family. Hank had refused to pay a ransom and had told the kidnappers he would never bend to blackmail. Still, these vague notes didn't come close to constituting proof that Chet Chandler knew about his sister's kidnapping.

But then Alex opened one last message. This one contained a video clip and took several seconds to load. A room came into view from the perspective of a camera mounted high in the corner looking down on the space. A woman sat in a chair in the middle of the room. Her ankles and wrists bore metal cuffs secured to the chair. And she was blindfolded. But Jim didn't have to see her entire face to know it was Lana.

He leaped to his feet. "Sonofa—" he exclaimed. Senator Chet Chandler was involved in his sister's kidnapping? He'd kill the guy. Or worse, expose him. He'd *ruin* the bastard. Nobody messed with his little sister and got away with it.

"Copy these files for me," Jim ground out. "I'll have them in front of a grand jury first thing in the morning."

"You can't," Alex replied. "We don't have a warrant to search this computer."

"Then get one!"

"By the time we get a judge to sign off on one, Chandler would hear about it and erase these before we ever get here."

"Make me a copy of the damned things anyway," Jim growled. "Illegally obtained or not, I want the evidence on the slime ball. I *will* find a way to take him down."

Without comment, Alex reached into her pocket for a flash drive. She plugged it into the side of the senator's computer and reached over Jim's shoulder to strike several keys. "Done."

"What else has Chandler got on this system?" Jim demanded.

"I don't—" She broke off as the outer office door beeped. "Get over on the couch," she whispered. "Write something down on this, fast." She threw him a yellow legal pad, slammed the screen on the laptop shut, and raced for the outer office door.

He heard her say pleasantly from the other room, "Hey, Parker. Mike said you'd stop by. How's Marly?"

Impressed, Jim listened to her and the guard chat about the guy's apparently about-to-have-a-baby wife. Man. Alex really was cool under pressure. The guard poked his head into the senator's office and Jim looked up from his legal pad casually. He nodded at the guard, who nodded back.

In a few moments, the fellow left and Alex came back into the office. She picked up where they'd left off. "Here's the thing," she explained. "If I copy the entire contents of the senator's hard drive, it'll only give us a snapshot of what's on the system this very minute. I'd rather have a way to track what he's doing from day-to-day."

"Can you do that?" Jim asked.

"I don't have the gear with me to do it tonight, but I can get the stuff and plant a transmitter on his motherboard. But I'll need to set up another computer somewhere nearby to act as the shadow system."

"Shadow system?"

She nodded. "The second computer will act exactly like the first computer. We'll see every keystroke the senator makes, every email he receives or sends, every file he opens, saves or deletes. Although, on our system, nothing will actually delete."

"Anyone ever tell you you're scary, Mendez?"

She smiled wolfishly. "All the time."

It was a quick matter to wipe down the senator's desk for fingerprints and turn out the lights. But Jim was surprised when she left the outer office lights on and then led him away from the elevator bank they'd used to come upstairs.

"What's up?" he murmured under his voice.

"We're supposed to be pulling an all-nighter working on a set of questions. Unless you want to sit in the office the rest of night, I thought we'd use the back door."

"But you said it would take an hour to get through its security."

"From the outside. From inside the building it's a two-minute job to disable the thing. Our only problems are Parker and the cleaning crew. I'll take point."

And just like that, she strode off down the hall, leaving him to follow behind. Memories of a dark, rocky valley flashed through his head. Another woman taking point. His misgivings about letting her do it, the rolled eyes of the other guys on the op, his determination to let her prove herself to the unit...

He shook his head and scowled at Alex's attempt to play toy soldier. She didn't get it at all. She had no idea how dangerous it was in the field and wasn't the slightest bit equipped to handle it, physically or emotionally.

She surprised him by hand-signaling a retreat, Special Forces style. His many years of training kicked in and he obeyed, not questioning the order. He turned, raced down the hall they currently were in, and ducked into the next available side hall. She joined him a second later. They froze in the shadowed alcove, shoulder to shoulder, as a janitor rolled a cleaning cart past them. The guy never saw them. A door opened and the cart creaked inside.

Alex glided out to the main hallway, peeked around the corner, and signaled him to proceed. Amusement flared in his gut. She had all the moves, he'd grant her that. But nobody was shooting at them or hunting them with the intent to kill. And that made all the difference between a real field op and this little pretend game of hers. But who was he to puncture her balloon? He dutifully followed her to the service exit and stood lookout while she disabled the door alarm.

She hadn't lied. In under two minutes they slipped out into the cool Washington night. He unclipped his badge and passed it to her to hand in to the security guard in the morning. They walked around the corner to his car. He drove away slowly enough not to draw any attention to himself; they were just another pair of weary staffers going home after burning the midnight oil.

But when they were safely a few blocks away, Jim pulled the car over and asked, "When can you have the senator's computer bugged?"

"Noon tomorrow."

"How so soon?" he demanded.

"I'll send the senator a virus in an email. It'll freeze up his system. He'll panic and call me into his office to fix it. I'll take apart the computer, wire the transmitter to the motherboard, and then erase the virus. No sweat."

Ballsy, to plant a bug right under her boss's nose. Jim nodded tersely. "I want to know everything. How involved is this guy in Lana's kidnapping? Who's he working with? Who did those emails come from? Particularly the one that told him to lean on my old man. If Chandler's just a pawn in this thing, I want to know who the king is."

"I'm going to need somewhere to set up the shadow computer. Somewhere close. Like an office or an apartment."

"I'll take care of it first thing in the morning," he replied tersely.

"What about a search warrant for Chet's computer?" she asked.

He shook his head. "No. You were right. We don't want to spook Chandler. I'll run the paperwork for your bug through military channels. The people who had me put you in Chandler's office can green-light us. And they won't leak anything."

She glanced over at him sharply, but then looked away hastily. Why had she gone skittish on him all of a sudden? "What?" he demanded.

"Us?" she mumbled. "Are you coming on board my op, then?"

"This scumbucket can lead me to Lana's kidnappers—or

he might even be one of them. Hell, yes, I'm in." He added grimly, "Call me when the bug's in place."

She nodded.

"You need a ride to your place?" he offered.

"It's too far out of your way," she protested.

"I'm wide awake and too pissed off at Chandler to go back to sleep any time soon."

"Fine. Then head south on I-395 to the Beltway."

He followed her directions to a nondescript apartment complex in suburban Virginia that looked like every other apartment complex around it. She reached for her door handle to jump out, and he stopped her with a hand on her left forearm.

"Hey, Al. Thanks. You did good tonight."

She nodded and then all but fell out of his car. He grinned. That girl was a mess. He drove home thoughtfully. Why on earth was Chet Chandler mixed up in something as dangerous and potentially career-ending as kidnapping?

Jim's gut said that Chet Chandler's strings were being pulled by the same person or persons the kidnappers had worked for. His father believed the Raven's Head Society was behind Lana's kidnapping. According to Hank, the Ravens included some of the richest, most powerful, most influential people on the planet. But then, according to Hank, the Ravens also had a plan to rule the world in secret.

Who was the unseen player pulling Chet Chandler's strings? All the signs pointed to there being one. Who in this town had the raw power to force United States senators to dance for them? What had Mendez stumbled into the middle of?

Chapter 2

It was a strange feeling planting a bug in a man's computer while he stood over her, watching. Not to mention the man being grateful to have her do it.

"What would I do without you, Alex?" Senator Chandler commented as he sat down at his now-functioning computer.

She laughed. "You'd be on a first-name basis with the Congressional I.T. support guys."

"You're way better than those idiots," Chandler declared. "And faster."

She shrugged modestly. *I ought to be better than those guys. I trained a bunch of them.* "Just give me a shout if it acts up again, sir."

She backed out of Chandler's office. It was likely he wouldn't notice her existence again until the next time his computer had a problem. She was good at being invisible. Of course, it was easy enough to do with everyone bustling around here as if the world would stop spinning if their current personal crisis didn't get solved in the next two minutes.

Come to think of it, she'd been pretty invisible on the ranch, too. She'd been just one of the passel of kids and puppies who'd run all over the place in the summers. She and Lana had been the only girls. But nobody had ever doubted that Lana was all girl. She wore pretty clothes and didn't like snakes or worms or touching fish, and she'd refused to roughhouse with her brothers. Alex had been willing to do any of that stuff if it meant she got to spend time with Jim Kelley. And then there was her dad, of course. After the accident, he'd never been the same...

"Thanks for working your magic, Alex," her supervisor in Chandler's office said warmly. "I owe you one."

Alex smiled. "Speaking of which, I've got a dentist appointment this afternoon. Will it be a problem for me to take a long lunch?"

The harassed chief-of-staff, Trevor McKinley, replied, "Are you kidding? You saved my life getting the boss's computer up and running again so fast. Take the rest of the day off."

Alex smiled and slipped out of the office. When she stepped onto the sidewalk, she pulled out her cell phone and called Jim's office extension.

"Captain Kelley," he answered shortly.

"Hi, it's me. I'm done."

"Perfect. Can I pick you up somewhere?"

She blinked, startled. He wanted to come get her? Vividly aware of not wanting to talk about sensitive information over an unsecured phone, she replied lightly, "How about I meet you?"

"Kirby's. Noon. Lunch," he bit out.

A lunch date with Jim Kelley? Holy cow. "Uhh, okay. See ya there." She disconnected the call in minor shock. It was just work, but still. She was having lunch with him! She glanced down at her clothes in dismay. She looked like a prison guard in these severe gray pants and white Oxford shirt. No help for it. She didn't have time to go home and make it back downtown before noon. So much for acting more like Lana Kelley. Abandoning the Beast in its outrageously expensive spot in the parking garage around the corner, she opted to grab the Metro to the other end of the Mall and Kirby's Diner.

When she walked into the crowded joint at five minutes till twelve, Jim was already there. She was thankful that he subscribed religiously to the army theory that if you weren't five minutes early, you were late. He spotted her and waved. Somehow, he'd managed to snag a postage-stamp-sized table that optimistically was supposed to seat two. She made her way through the noisy crush to join him.

She sat down and gulped as her knee promptly banged into his. She levered herself sideways to avoid physical contact with him. No way could she eat a messy hamburger while rubbing knees with the man. She'd choke to death for sure. She picked up the glass of ice water he'd already ordered for her and took a sip.

"How was your morning?" he asked.

"Productive. Yours?" she replied more breathlessly than she liked.

"The same." Grinning, he reached into his pocket and fished out a set of keys. "Here."

"What are these?"

"Keys to the love nest you and I are about to borrow on Capitol Hill for a little while."

She inhaled sharply, which was unfortunate given that she was still sipping at her water. She coughed violently enough that Jim reached around to thump her on the back, which didn't do a darned thing to help her breathe.

"Jeez. Don't say things like that to a girl when she's drinking."

Abruptly grim, he murmured under the din around them, "We're green-lighted."

"For what?"

"Full-blown op. Looks like you're finally going to get your wish to play soldier, and I'm going to get mine to go after Lana's kidnappers."

She jolted. *He doesn't know about all the things I've done to finagle working with him, does he?* Belatedly, she realized he was talking about their argument yesterday. She scowled. "I still want to go to a war zone. Experience real combat. A 'love nest' on Capitol Hill hardly qualifies."

"I dunno. The halls of power in this town can be pretty cutthroat."

She rolled her eyes as a waitress came to take their orders and left again.

Jim leaned close. "Whatever you want, you've got it. Sky's the limit."

If only.

"Any gear, any cool gadgets you need. Just say the word."

Whoopee. Gadgets.

"The place is furnished. All we've got to do is move in and go for it."

Does he have to keep saying things like that? I'd love nothing better than to go for it with him.

"You think you're up to this, Al?"

"Uhh. Yeah. Sure."

"I can't wait to nail that guy."

I can't wait to nail him. *Oh, wait. Work. This is the mission I've been dreaming of getting. Minus the war zone. But hey. It's a start.*

Their lunch arrived and she stared down in dismay at the juicy burger, piled high with all the trimmings. She doubted she could get her mouth around that thing, let alone do it in either a neat or ladylike fashion.

Abandoning fashion for common sense, she unfolded her napkin and tucked it into the front of her shirt before she tackled the hamburger. Jim grinned and did the same. But then, he was wearing a three-hundred-dollar silk tie.

"When do you have to get back to the office?" he asked just as she took a bite of her sandwich.

She chewed convulsively. *Don't choke. Don't choke. Don't choke.* Finally, she was able to answer safely, "Tomorrow morning. Trevor gave me the rest of the day off."

"Who's Trevor?"

Stunned, Alex stared at him. He sounded a shade defensive there for a second. "My boss. Chandler's chief of staff."

"Ahh."

To Alex's immense relief, they ate in silence after that. The last thing she needed was for Jim to have to give her the Heimlich maneuver and for her to spew half-chewed hamburger all over the place.

"Did you drive?" he asked after he casually flipped a couple of bills on the table to cover the meal and a hefty tip.

"No. The Beast is still up on the Hill."

"Why do you keep that thing anyway?"

Because her father had saved his money for a year to buy the wreck and the two of them had fixed it up together the first winter after her brother died. She was fairly certain the car had saved her brokenhearted father's life. And then he'd given it to her when she graduated from high school.... Its sentimental value was beyond price.

"It still runs. Why would I get rid of a perfectly functional car?" she demanded.

He shrugged. "Guess I'm driving then."

They got into his sexy little Beemer—how did he manage to keep getting plum parking spots like that?—and headed out.

Of course, the love nest came with underground parking for two. The Beast was going to adore getting to sit beside Jim's sleek sports car. The building also had a weight room, hot tub and indoor swimming pool, but she doubted she and Jim would be making much use of those facilities.

The building manager gave them each key cards to the building, their own security codes, and introduced them to the doorman. Finally, they were shown up to their borrowed flat and left alone.

The place wasn't as posh as Jim's house, but then he'd no doubt had some fancy decorator with an unlimited budget do his place. But it was a whole lot nicer than her apartment, and the furniture all matched. More to the point, it was less than three blocks from the Dirksen Building, well within the range of the bug she'd planted in the senator's laptop.

"It only has one bedroom," she accused. With an obscenely huge bed, no less.

"What part of *love nest* don't you grasp?" he replied.

She glared at him and changed the subject. "How in the heck am I supposed to sneak my gear up here past all those doormen and security cameras?"

"I'll help you carry it up. We'll bring it up in pieces if we have to."

"Oh, we'll have to, all right."

"Don't worry about it. I've got your back, kid."

She really wished he'd quit calling her that. It made her feel about twelve years old. But she supposed it was better than Al. That's what he called her around the battalion when he wasn't bellowing out her last name at her. She sighed. How did Lana Kelley so effortlessly keep her female identity around all those guys on the ranch? Every summer, when the time drew near for the arrival of the Kelley kids for their annual summer sojourn in Montana, she'd dreaded Lana's arrival nearly as much as she'd anticipated Jim's.

It took the rest of the afternoon for them to shuttle electronic surveillance equipment from the battalion to Jim's car, and from his car to the love nest, disguised in cardboard boxes he took delight in labeling things such as Naughty Lingerie and Miscellaneous Toys.

By supper time, she had an elaborate computer system up and running on the desk in the corner of the living room—the shadow system to Chet Chandler's—and a second one to record and backup everything from the first one.

"Does it work?" Jim asked over her shoulder as she typed in the senator's password to activate the system.

"Of course it works," she replied scornfully. "I built it."

"Now what?"

"Now we watch what Chet does. He's checking his calendar right now."

It was a little eerie watching commands and words scroll across her screen as if a ghost were typing on her keyboard.

"So, just out of curiosity," she asked, "is this a legal wiretap, or is it completely off the books?"

"Both. My superiors have declared this a Homeland Security investigation, which means we have permission to pretty well stomp all over the good senator's constitutional privacy rights. But it's definitely way off the books. We don't know how deep into the government whoever's controlling Chet has their hooks. Only a handful of people have any idea what you and I are doing."

"Heck, *I* don't have any idea what we're doing. For months I've been working for the senator and I still have no idea what I'm supposed to be looking for."

"Have you got a white-noise maker?" he asked quietly.

She frowned. "We've already swept the place for bugs or cameras."

"I know." He gave her a sober look.

Well, okay then. "Lemme go get it." It took her several minutes of digging around in her "Boring Underwear" box to find the darned thing, but she brought the noisemaker into the living room and plugged it in. She threw Jim an expectant look.

He gestured for her to sit on the other end of the sofa from him. Even with the electronic interference of her gadget all around them, he still spoke barely above a whisper. What on earth could be making the man this paranoid?

"We have reason to believe that Senator Chandler is part of a large-scale conspiracy. The same one that nearly killed my father."

"How's Hank doing by the way? Any change?"

"No. They've still got him in the induced coma until the swelling in his brain comes down some more. We were hoping he could tell us exactly who's involved in this conspiracy, or at least who threatened him when Lana was kidnapped. It may be a while yet before he can talk...assuming he remembers anything at all when he wakes up."

"What does Lana have to do with this conspiracy thing?" Alex asked, startled.

"We believe whoever kidnapped her did it to force my father into cooperating with this group. Maybe they needed him to do something for them."

"Why couldn't they get some other congressman to do their dirty work for them? Why him?" Alex asked.

Jim shrugged. "Until he wakes up and can tell us that, your guess is as good as mine. Lord knows, my old man is no saint."

That wasn't news to her. But it was hard to imagine him lying unconscious in a hospital bed. He'd always been so loud and forceful and dynamic. As a kid, she'd been more than a little afraid of him.

"What do you know about this conspiracy?" she asked.

"Precious little. We know they recruit rich and powerful people. They probably hide their money behind some corporate shell company."

"What do they want?"

"In a word—power."

She sighed. "Them and everyone else in this town."

"I'm talking serious power. Way beyond what some elected schmuck can gather in a few terms on the right committees. I'm talking running nations. Taking down world leaders if they feel like it. Starting wars. Or ending them."

Whoa. He was talking *Power* with a capital *P*. "So we're looking for links to these guys in Senator Chandler's computer? Have you got a name? Anything?"

"Nope. We're running blind."

Good thing he had her, then. Her job was to give eyes and ears—real-time, usable intelligence—to operators in the field. "All right then. Let's take a look at Chet's email correspondence. If we don't find anything there, how about we move on to a list of his biggest donors? Stands to reason if he's in someone's back pocket, that person is paying to keep the senator in office."

Jim nodded. "The money's probably coming in privately or through some network of cover corporations."

She grinned. "That would be why I've got the second computer here. How about I surf the internet and see what I can scare up on his various donors? Maybe I can find connections between some of them."

"Have at it. I hate to abandon you, but I've got to get back to the office. Delta Company's about to touch down in Africa and I need to get their initial threat assessment."

She sighed. "Rub salt in the wound, will ya?"

"Get over it, Mendez."

Heck, she'd been trying to get over *him* for the past fifteen years to no avail. What made him think she was going to get over her goal to experience combat up close and personal any time soon? *As if.*

Chapter 3

Jim paused outside the door of the love nest, supper in hand. How weird was this, posing as lover to Alex? Hell, it made him hinky even to think about her being a girl. She'd always been Arturo's kid sister, and then she'd been the resident tomboy on the ranch. Not to mention she was one of his troops now, too—even if she was only on loan to his unit. She was practically one of the guys, for God's sake. His Kelley family loyalty was torn—catch Lana's kidnappers or put Alex in danger. How was he supposed to choose?

He pushed the door open and, no surprise, Alex was seated in front of the second computer. "Hi, honey. I'm home."

She made a rude remark any one of his soldiers might have made to him and kept typing.

He laughed and went into the tiny kitchen. "I hope you like Chinese. I picked up takeout for us."

"Give me the one with beef."

"How'd you know I got one with beef?" he challenged.

"Your family owns a cattle ranch in Montana. It's your duty to support the beef industry."

He grinned and carried the white cardboard box to her. "Beef and broccoli."

"Thanks."

"Find anything?" he asked from the armchair across the room.

"Maybe. The senator is going to a fundraiser tomorrow night hosted by some company called the McNaught Group. Ever hear of them?"

"No. Should I have?"

She shrugged. "You'd have to run in the right circles to come across them."

He frowned. What was that supposed to mean?

She continued, "They describe themselves as a strategic analysis and investment group. Whatever the heck that is. But what's interesting is several of their board members are donors to the Chandler campaign. Why would east-coast power brokers give a darn about the junior senator from Nebraska?"

"Good question."

"I did a little digging on McNaught's finances and ran into a whole bunch of nesting corporations. A dozen or more of them lead back to other Chandler donors."

"Any way you can tell if they contributed to my dad's campaign?"

"I'd have to get a list of your father's campaign contributors. I don't know if that's readily available public information."

He made a face. "I know just the person to get it for us."

"Who?"

"Who else? My mother."

"Really. You don't have to call her. I don't want to put you in an uncomfortable situation with your family."

"Just because she's divorcing Hank, that doesn't mean she isn't as interested as I am in catching whoever kidnapped her baby girl. She'll help me."

Alex chose that moment to spill her beef and broccoli all over her shirt. Red-faced, she made a dash for the bathroom. He pulled out his cell phone. "Hi, Mom. How are you doing tonight?"

Sarah Mistler Kelley sounded as composed as she always did. "I'm fine, dear. Is there any change in his condition?"

No need to ask who she meant. She might have left Hank because of his mistresses, but she'd loved the man and had had six children with him. Jim answered her regretfully, "No change. They're still waiting for the brain swelling to come down so they can let him regain consciousness. The doctors said it could be a week or more. We just have to be patient."

A sigh came through the line. "Thanks for the update."

"Actually, that's not why I called."

"Oh?"

"I'm looking into who kidnapped Lana. Just poking around informally to make sure the police are doing their job. I was wondering if you have a list of campaign donors from Dad's last couple of elections."

"Of course. I had to put together all the seating charts at the fundraisers and send out the thank-you notes. I can email the lists to you if you like."

"That would be great."

By the time Alex emerged from the bedroom wearing jeans and a maroon Harvard T-shirt, he was seated at her computer, logged on to his email and printing out the donor list, which had already come through from Sarah. Efficient woman, his mother.

"Ask and ye shall receive," he told Alex as he handed over the list.

She nodded and jerked a thumb at him to get out of her seat. Grinning, he moved aside.

"Want a beer?" he asked.

She threw him a strangely hurt look. "No, thank you."

What was up with that? He'd seen her hoist a cold one with the guys in the unit plenty of times before. Whatever. He turned on the world news to see if there was any new pirate activity being reported in the Sea of Aden. It was a sad but true fact that he got nearly as much of his intelligence on world events from the news channels as he did through classified military means.

Alex worked through the evening, surfing and scribbling. Finally, at about ten o'clock, she pushed her chair back and rubbed the back of her neck.

"Need me to work out that kink?" he offered.

She jolted so hard she all but fell out of her chair. "No. I got it."

"Find anything?"

"Maybe. Yes. I think so."

"What've you got?"

He plugged in the white-noise machine as she moved over to the sofa and spread her notes out on the coffee table. "At least twenty of the same corporate donors and another dozen large private donors contributed to both your father's and Chet's last campaigns. These folks have donated to Chandler's last several campaigns, but they were all first-time donors to your dad's last campaign."

He frowned, staring at the lengthy list of names. He'd never heard his father mention any of these people. "I don't think any of these guys are from California."

"I know they're not." She shrugged. "Your father and Chandler both tend to vote conservatively, so these donors could conceivably just be supporting like-minded senatorial candidates. Or, they could've bought Chet a while back and just be getting around to buying your father. How'd Hank's last campaign go?"

"It was a close thing. His conservative platform doesn't always play well with west-coast voters. He was behind in all the polls throughout the campaign and forecasted by everyone to lose. Then he got a big influx of cash at the last minute and was able to blitz the media with family-values ads." He added bitterly, "Which we all know now to be a load of crap."

Alex replied quietly, "Just because he cheated on his wife doesn't mean he doesn't love his kids."

Jim shrugged. "He's not the man I thought he was." He figured Alex would know what he was talking about. She'd grown up around Hank and seen how larger-than-life but out of reach the man had always been, especially in the eyes of his sons.

"Lots of people aren't the same as they appear on the surface."

She sounded oddly choked up when she said that. He studied her closely, but her dark eyes gave away nothing. But then she cleared her throat and said briskly, "Almost every donor on that list is going to be at Senator Chandler's fundraiser tomorrow night."

"The one this McNaught Group is putting on?" Jim asked. She nodded.

"Then I guess I'm going to have to get myself invited to it," he commented.

"How?" Alex blurted.

"Easy. I'll call and tell them I want to give Chandler money."

She replied doubtfully, "The guest list is pretty exclusive. Some of the richest people in this part of the country are going."

"All the more reason to be there. Sounds like exactly the kind of people I'm looking for."

She said hesitantly, "I don't know if you're rich enough to get in. And the cost per plate is thirty thousand dollars."

He shrugged. "We can always have Homeland Security add a few zeroes to my bank-account totals if it turns out I'm not wealthy enough to get in on my own."

She blinked, stunned. "They can do that?"

He laughed. "I wasn't kidding when I said you and I can have whatever we want on this op. The people who put me on this job seriously want to see this bunch of folks exposed."

"Wow."

"I'll arrange for the boost to my bank accounts in the morning. And you'd better call in sick for work tomorrow."

She stared at him. "Why?"

"Because you have to go shopping."

"For what?"

"A decent dress to wear to the McNaught fundraiser with me."

"What?" she squawked.

"Do you even own a dress, Mendez?"

"Of course," she answered quickly enough that he wondered if she was telling the truth.

"It'll need to be a fancy one. The McNaught fundraiser is no doubt black-tie."

"As in tuxedos and ball gowns?" she practically squeaked.

"Exactly."

She subsided, looking horrified. He laughed. "Chin up, kid. If you're nice to me I won't take blackmail pictures of you in a dress to post in the unit."

"Try it and I'll have to get even with you."

"How do you figure you'll do that?"

"I'll tell everyone about you kissing the goat."

Laughter rolled through him. "Lord, I haven't thought about that in years. The Colton twins dared me to do it."

"The way I heard it, they didn't dare you to do it at the

summer dance. Taking that poor goat as your date was purely your idea. I can't wait to see what the guys in the unit do when they find out you make out with goats," she gloated.

He groaned. "Okay, fine. No pictures tomorrow. Truce?" He held out a hand to shake on the deal.

She reached for his hand but failed to take into account the coffee table between them and pitched over it into the sofa. Fortunately, the piece was overstuffed and broke her fall without injury.

"Remind me to wear body armor under my tux tomorrow night," he declared. "I'm going to need it if I'm going to dance with you."

Her response was muffled by the sofa cushions, but given the irritation in her voice, he was glad he couldn't make out the words.

"I'm heading home, Mendez. Give me a call in the morning if you come up with anything new overnight."

Something unrepeatable floated out of the sofa pillow. Laughing quietly, he walked out the door.

Alex stared at the closed door and all but burst into tears. When was she going to stop turning into a complete klutz every time he touched her or walked into the room with her?

A black-tie dinner dance, huh? With Jim Kelley? She was so hosed. The only dress she owned was the one she'd worn to her uncle's funeral a few years ago, and it had managed to be out of style even then.

Desperate, she picked up her phone and made a panicked call. "Carla, you've got to save my life."

She'd gone to high school with Carla Grant back in Maple Cove and the young woman had come to town recently to work in the new Washington, D.C., office of Walsh Enterprises, an oil and gas exploration company headquartered back in Montana.

"What's up, Alex?" Carla laughed. "Did you get lost in a department store and accidentally wander into the women's clothing section? Remember, you get your clothes in men's wear."

"Very funny. That's my problem. I've got to get a dress. A long one. For a fancy dance. I have to do makeup and everything. And, ohmigosh, my hair. I can't wear a ponytail to this thing."

"Whoa! You have a *date?* With a living, breathing man? Spill, girlfriend."

Alex scowled. "I've been invited to a fundraiser for the senator I work for."

"By whom? Not one of those gay Congressional staffers using you to convince people they're straight?" Carla demanded.

"No. Jim Kelley."

Silence came from the other end of the line. Had she given Carla a no-kidding heart attack? "Did I kill you?" Alex asked anxiously as the silence stretched out.

An ear-splitting scream erupted in her ear, making Alex yank the phone away from her head. From arm's length, she still heard Carla squeal, "Tell me *everything!*"

"There's not much to tell. He's going to a fundraiser and had to bring a guest. I guess he's between blonde confections right now and had to grab the first available female on short notice. Or maybe the last available female," she added a little sourly.

"When's this big event of yours?" Carla demanded, getting down to the serious business of date preparation.

"Tomorrow night."

"Oh my God. Call in sick tomorrow. I'll do the same. This is going to take us all day."

"How long does it *take* to shop for one lousy dress, anyway?" Alex asked in alarm.

"It's not just a dress. There are the shoes and lingerie and makeup and hair, the mani-pedi—"

Alex made a sound of distress.

"—don't you worry. Leave it all to me."

Like Alex had any choice. She was completely clueless about all this girl stuff. Her mother had taken off when she was an infant and she'd only had her dad and a ranch full of cowboys to raise her. Which had been bad enough. But when Arturo had died, everything had changed.

It wasn't as if she'd had any choice but to try to step into her dead brother's shoes. Her father was so distraught she'd been terrified she'd lose him, too. If becoming her older brother in every way she could manage saved her dad, she'd been willing to do it. Even if it had cost her dresses and dating and growing gracefully into a young woman.

She'd even gone into the army, like Arturo was supposed to do. And the army wasn't exactly a bastion of instruction in the feminine arts. She'd gotten her college degree mostly online while she bounced around from army post to army post, secretly trying to catch up with Jim Kelley.

Even the assignment to Chandler's office hadn't helped much. The man had only a few female staffers, and rumor had it they were on staff only because of old charges of sexism against Chet. The women in Chandler's office were so busy proving they were as good as the boys that they didn't wallow in things feminine much, either.

"I'll be there at 10:00 a.m. sharp," Carla announced, breaking Alex's gloomy train of thought. "That's when the malls open."

"Right. Ten o'clock." She gave Carla quick instructions to the love nest and then added, "Thanks, Carla."

"Hey. What are friends for?"

Chapter 4

After three solid hours of shopping with Carla, Alex was beginning to have deep reservations about her friend. The woman was a slave driver. Who knew this business of girly primping was so darned much work?

At least she had a moment to catch her breath while two nice ladies administered her first ever mani-pedi. So this was what it was like to be a girl, huh? She had to admit it was nice. But she would never tell that to Carla, of course. Although, how she was going to type with French-tipped fingernails was anybody's guess.

Carla pulled out an actual checklist and glanced through it again. "Hair's in twenty minutes. You can eat while your highlights go in. I can't believe you only gave me one day to work a miracle, Alex. What were you thinking?"

Alex winced. "He asked me last night. I didn't get any more warning than you."

"Well, at least the dress is a knock-out. Jim Kelley's not going to know what hit him."

And neither would her bank account when that credit card came due. But the dress really was stunning. It was red, of course. With her honey-hued skin and dark hair, that was a no-brainer. How the gown managed to be slinky and classy at the same time was a mystery to her, though. Carla declared it the result of a great designer. Alex just knew she'd never felt so pretty…or feminine.

She was abjectly grateful when Carla took over the conversation with the hairdresser. They got going about highlights and lowlights and she was dead lost by the time they got to layers and weight around her face. Who knew hair had weight?

Carla was fretting by the time they got back to the love nest at four o'clock, fussing that they barely had time to dress her before Jim came at seven to pick her up.

"Wow. Nice place," Carla commented as Alex let her into the flat. She'd mentioned to Jim that she was inviting an old girlfriend over as part of establishing the cover of living there and he hadn't objected. And Carla couldn't tell the business end of a computer any more than Alex could tell the business end of a mascara brush, as it turned out.

The next hour was spent in the bathroom with abundant laughter from Carla and abundant cursing from Alex.

"Okay, Alex. Watch carefully. You roll the mascara brush like this. It separates your lashes and gives them more volume."

She got the hang of putting on makeup eventually, and she had to admit that when it was all said and done, she didn't look like a slutty raccoon as she'd feared she would. In fact, her brown eyes looked huge and dramatic, and her smile looked, well, amazing.

"I can't believe that's me," she breathed into the mirror. Her dark hair draped around her face and over her shoulders in lush waves that made her look exotic and sexy. Totally un-Alex.

"Oh, it's you, all right," Carla declared. "I've been saying all along you'd clean up great if you'd just give it a try. Let's go zip you into your dress. Can I leave it to you to put on your own shoes before Jim gets here?"

Alex stuck her tongue out at her friend. Putting the shoes on wasn't what worried her. Walking in them was. The strappy stilettos had at least three-inch heels, and she was going to be within a hundred yards of Jim Kelley—a deadly combination.

In a few minutes, she stood in front of the full-length mirror in the walk-in closet, simply staring.

"Don't you cry on me, Alex Mendez. I worked too hard getting that makeup just right on you. And don't kid yourself. It may be waterproof mascara, but it'll still run down your chin and give you a fake beard if you boo-hoo enough."

Alex blinked away the tears in her eyes and hugged her friend. "You're the best, Carla."

"Of course I am. That's why I'm your friend. I'm going to skedaddle before Tall, Dark, and Gorgeous gets here. But you have to *swear* to tell me how he reacts when he sees you. That boy's going to have a cow. Although, as I recall, goats are more his style," Carla laughed.

Alex grinned. "I mentioned that last night. May I recommend you not bring it up in his presence? Apparently, he's still a little touchy on the subject of dating ba-a-a-ah-d girls."

Laughing, Carla fetched her purse. "Call me tomorrow. Promise?"

"Promise."

Alex had barely enough time after letting out Carla to go back to the bedroom, check her lipstick, which was supposedly some sort of long-lasting stain, and smooth her gown down her body before she heard a key in the front door.

"Ready to go, Mendez?" Jim called from the living room.

She picked up the red, crystal-covered clutch with her emergency makeup in it and stepped out of the bedroom.

Jim Kelley was a hard man to shock speechless, but when Alex Mendez appeared wearing the sexiest red dress he'd ever seen, damned if speech didn't desert him entirely. His gaze slid all the way down to her painted toenails and back up past the sexy skirt slit with a slender, tanned leg peeking out of it, past the low-cut top—and hitching for a moment on the provocative cleavage—to the lush waves of hair, and finally her face. With *makeup*. Cripes, she looked like a movie star.

"Mendez?" he finally choked out. "What happened to you?"

She blinked, alarmed. "Why? Is something wrong? You said it was formal." She ran a panicked hand down the clingy fabric of her dress.

"Hell, no. Nothing's wrong. You look…" He struggled for a word and finally settled on "…magnificent. Incredible. Are you sure I can't take a picture? The guys will never believe me—"

"No pictures!" she blurted.

He supposed he could understand her not wanting the Neanderthals at the office harassing her for impersonating a girl. Although, as impersonations went, this one was pretty damned spectacular. Gussied up, Alex Mendez was *beautiful*.

A slow smile spread across his face as he formally offered her his arm. He asked politely, "Are you ready to go, Alex? We wouldn't want to be late."

Hesitantly, she laid her hand on his forearm, and he waited for her to fall over. But shockingly, she remained upright. She took a cautious step. Another. Normally, he'd make a sarcastic comment about her walking upright for a change, but suddenly, picking on her felt weird. Not nearly as weird as the idea that Mendez was a hot chick, though.

Her dad would be so proud of her. And Arturo—He broke off that train of thought sharply, but it insisted on completing itself. Arturo should've been alive to see this day. To see his little sister grow up into a beautiful woman. Jim shook his head. She looked so much like him it hurt. She shared some of Arturo's demons, too, apparently. His gut twisted. He might not have been able to save her brother from himself, but he would damn well save her.

Bedeviled by grim thoughts, he only belatedly noticed that they made it all the way down to his BMW, which was double-parked out front, without mishap. He hovered protectively as he tucked her into his car and made sure her gown wouldn't get caught in the door. During the short drive to the swanky hotel hosting the event, he glanced over at her every minute or two.

Finally, Alex demanded, "What's wrong? You're acting like I've sprouted a second head."

He jerked his gaze back to the road. "Not at all. I just can't get over how great you look. I'm trying to figure out how I missed it all these years."

He supposed that would've involved him really looking at her. But how did you look someone in the eye when you'd killed their brother? Sure, the police had ruled it all an unfortunate accident. And yeah, he'd told Arturo to quit screwing around and sit down and buckle his seat belt. And no one could've known those deer would jump out in front of the truck, or that the road would be a touch icy in that spot. Or that the truck would careen off an embankment and plunge nearly fifty feet into a ravine—

She mumbled, sounding disgruntled, "I'm not a blonde."

"I beg your pardon?"

Alex shrugged, "You always go for blondes. Even that poor goat was a blonde. I'm not your type. That's why you don't notice me."

Guilt kicked him in the solar plexus. Hell, now he was giving her a complex on top of killing her brother. "Alex, you're *any* man's type. Women don't come too much more beautiful or sexy than you. You're going to turn every head at the ball."

She rolled her eyes at him, but he meant it. She was a knockout.

He pulled up in front of the hotel and flipped his keys and a hefty tip to the valet, who also seemed to be having trouble tearing his gaze away from Alex.

As the Beemer pulled away, Jim held his arm out to her once more. "Shall we?" he murmured, smiling warmly.

A slow, answering smile unfolded on her face and Jim caught his breath. The woman just kept getting more gorgeous the longer he looked at her.

He hadn't overstated the reaction other men would have to her. Indeed, heads turned as the two of them stepped into the ballroom. A gray-haired man Jim didn't recognize closed in on them immediately. "Welcome, Mr. Kelley. Glad to have you join us tonight."

Slick operators, these McNaught people, to be able to identify him on sight with less than one day's notice. "Call me Jim," he replied smoothly. "Thanks for having me on such short notice. I'm excited to contribute to getting Senator Chandler back in Congress for another term. Chet and I see eye-to-eye on so many things. It's nice to know my interests are being looked out for on Capitol Hill."

"You're Hank Kelley's boy, aren't you? How's he doing?"

Jim answered grimly, "He's still in a coma. No sign of a recovery." And if these bastards were the ones who'd shot him, Jim would personally see to it they regretted it for the rest of their unnaturally short lives.

The guy actually slapped Jim's back. "So, Jim. Tell me more about you. What business are you in?"

"Businesses, plural," Jim replied, shrugging. "A little of this and that. Ranching, oil, gold, precious commodities. Whatever makes me money and a lot of it."

"Not risk-averse, are you?" their escort asked.

Jim laughed. "Caution is for the weak or uninformed."

Another man joined them and the first one commented, "We were just talking about investments."

The second man asked, "So why this particular fundraiser, Mr. Kelley? I understand you pulled a lot of strings to buy last-minute tickets."

"I'm interested in McNaught. Tonight's party gave me an opportunity to kill two birds with one stone. Support the Chandler campaign and finally meet the McNaught powers-that-be."

"For what purpose, Mr. Kelley?" the second man asked a little too casually.

He chose to misunderstand the fellow. "Why, to get Chet Chandler reelected, of course. Isn't that why we're all here?"

"Of course," both men replied, flashing him plastic smiles in unison. Not long after that, the men drifted away. Jim repeated the same conversation with only small variations, no less than a half dozen more times before dinner was served.

As the crowd abandoned its cocktails to be seated and eat undercooked scallops and overcooked filet mignon, he glanced down at Alex. "You're being awfully quiet."

"Observing."

He asked through his smile, "See anything interesting?"

"Definitely. We'll talk later."

He leaned down and all but put his mouth on her ear. "That sounds perfect."

She tilted her head toward him and murmured back without moving her lips, "Hidden cameras. Microphones or lip readers or both. Watch what you say."

He replied, "Guess I'll just have to spend the rest of the evening telling you how beautiful and sexy you are." Her eyes widened in something approaching shock, and he added, "You've got to get over acting surprised. People will think something's wrong with you if you don't take the compliments as your due. Try to act at home in your skin, darling."

"Easier said than done, snookums."

He laughed. "I like this look on you. You should stick with it."

"Have you seen who I work with?" she retorted.

He grinned ruefully at her. "For the record, they'd all love you like this."

"For the *record,* I'd never hear the end of it if I showed up at the office looking like this."

"Would that be so bad?" he asked half-seriously.

She caught the change of mood and considered. "Maybe. I don't know. I'd have to think about it."

Dinner was innocent enough. They were seated with various high-power business people and just plain rich folks, and the McNaught representative at their table didn't ply Jim with any probing questions. Chet Chandler gave a predictable and thoroughly boring speech. No wonder he needed McNaught's money to get himself reelected. The guy was as inspiring as dirty dishwater.

After dessert, waiters rapidly disassembled the tables and hauled them out while a swing band set up on the stage, transforming the venue into a dance.

And that was when the sharks closed in on Alex. There were plenty of harrumphing wives keeping husbands anchored firmly to their sides, but a solid third of the crowd was single, or at least unattached tonight, males. And they had no compunction about moving in on the stunning brunette and flirting her up. It was enough to make a guy a little defensive and a lot territorial.

The first time a slick lawyer from a major international law firm tried to get her phone number, Jim was surprised when Alex flashed him a faintly alarmed look and leaned in closer to him. His arm just naturally went around her shoulder to hug her to his side. Belatedly, he told himself it was what he would have done had she been Lana and some creep moved in on her. But Lana had Deacon now, and the guy was a professional mercenary. He doubted anyone would be moving in on his little sister any time soon.

Meanwhile, Alex seemed genuinely rattled by the aggressive male attention coming her way. After a drunk CEO blatantly tried to proposition her, Alex fled to the restroom and hid there until Jim called in through the door, "He's gone Alex. You can come out now."

She emerged sheepishly, her face a perfect match for her scarlet dress.

"You okay?" he asked.

"I'll live."

"There's one sure way to get rid of these jokers, you know," he said.

"Do tell."

"Dance with me."

She smiled ruefully. "They'll take one look at what a klutz I am and run screaming, huh?"

He placed his hand in the small of her back and guided her toward the large dance floor. "No. They'll figure out the lady's taken."

"But I'm not—"

He cut her off gently. "They only have to think you are."

"And how do I accomplish that?" she demanded.

"Follow my lead." He swept her into his arms and spun her

around once. And then he pulled her against him, plastering her body against his and—

Whoa. The woman was screaming hot. Her curves fit against his in all the right places, and in her nervous tension, she all but vibrated against him. The sexual energy thrumming through her roared through him.

His mind was completely blown. This was *Alex Mendez.* Suddenly and completely without warning, she'd gone from one of the guys, kid sister and tomboy to all woman. He had no idea what to think about that, but he knew one thing for sure. She felt pretty damned good in his arms.

As if he deserved to derive one single ounce of happiness from being with her. He was a royal jerk. The Mendez family owed him nothing.

His arm must've tightened more than he'd intended, crushing her against him, because she gasped in surprise.

Startled, he glanced down at her.

Her lush lips had parted and her eyes widened. As he watched, mesmerized, she ran the tip of her tongue over her lips, moistening them to kiss-me-now-you-fool status.

Stop thinking like that! he shouted at himself inside his head.

"That's better," he ground out. "Now you look like a woman in love."

Chapter 5

Alex froze in Jim's arms. *Ho. Lee. Crap.* She wasn't supposed to look in love with him! That was her secret, never, ever to be shared or revealed to him, or anyone else for that matter. *Think about something else. The weather. The stock market. Starving children in Africa!* It didn't help. She was in love with him and dancing in his arms, darn it. How was she supposed to think about anything else?

She'd fantasized about a moment exactly like this for years. Her all gussied up and ravishingly beautiful, him all gussied up and incapable of taking his eyes or hands off her. A fancy ball, dim lights and just the two of them gazing at one another and dancing the night away.

He was leading her carefully around the dance floor and holding her as if he thought she'd fall on her face if he held her any less tightly. He dragged her through her momentary fantasy-induced paralysis.

"Hey," she finally managed to respond with fake cheer,

"I'm supposed to look besotted with you. It's my job. Act like the girlfriend, right?"

He cleared his throat. "Uhh, right. Exactly."

She shouldn't have done it, but this was a once-in-a-lifetime opportunity. She let her hand stray from his shoulder to the back of his neck, her fingertips playing with the short hairs there. In response, his right hand strayed from her waist down toward the higher curves of her buttocks. She lifted her face to breathe gently on his neck; he tilted his head down to murmur compliments against her temple. She gazed up into his eyes, and he stared back, his sapphire eyes more turbulent and thoughtful than she'd expected. His intense expression unnerved her, sending strange tingles jangling through her body.

He's only pretending. This was a job for him, too. She was his cover so he could approach the McNaught people. Nothing more. But her body wasn't paying the slightest attention to her brain. Her breathing insisted on running fast and shallow, and she continued to feel hot and trembly all over.

The music shifted to something slow and slinky with a lot of wailing saxophone in it. The older couples mostly left the floor, and any appropriate distance between the younger couples disappeared. Jim's arm tightened around her waist, not only drawing her closer, but higher up against him until she was barely resting any weight on her toes. The fingers of his left hand twined with hers to drape her right arm over his shoulder. His palm slid down the length of her arm, passing perilously close to her breast as it traveled down her ribs. As if tingling for him wasn't bad enough, now she was shivering, too.

She had to get a grip…and not of his rear end as she was aching to do. Sure, she'd imagined a moment like this with this man forever. The best bet was to enjoy every moment of it but never to forget this was a one-time good deal. She never had been Jim Kelley's type, and just because she'd suddenly worn a dress and put on some makeup didn't mean she'd magically morphed into his dream girl.

But still…the reality of him was bigger, stronger and definitely more overwhelming than she'd pictured. If she hadn't been head over heels for him before, she would certainly be that way now. She would remember this night, this moment, for the rest of her life.

"You're frowning," he murmured. "Not enjoying yourself?"

"On the contrary. I'm lov—" she started. The words were out of her mouth before she could call them back. *Oh, Lord. Please let him not have heard her slip.*

A slow, smoky smile lit his eyes, traveling by degrees to the rest of his face. Crud. He'd heard. Mortified, she buried her face in the crook of his neck and steadfastly refused to look at him any more.

The dance ended and he led her off the floor. She was thankful that he wanted to work the room a bit, to stroll around introducing himself to various high rollers and greeting a few he already knew. Sometimes Alex forgot that he was a wealthy man in his own right and might actually know some of these power players.

She wasn't called upon to do much besides act as arm candy. Under normal circumstances she'd be insulted to be so completely ignored and marginalized by these men. But as it was, she had plenty of opportunity to study the people in the room and observe their interactions closely.

Yet another cluster of tuxedoed men loomed before them and Alex pasted on a fake smile as Jim approached them.

"Good grief, is that you, Alex?" one of the men exclaimed.

She jolted as Chet Chandler emerged from the crowd of men, looking shocked. "Uh, hi, sir. How'd your computer hold up today?"

"Fine, Alex. Well, would you look at you? I had no idea…"

She smiled. Didn't know how to finish that sentence, huh? Give the man brownie points for tact.

"Why haven't you ever…" he trailed off again.

"Come to the office looking like this?" she finished wryly.

"Well, yes."

"I wouldn't want to be a distraction to the important work at hand," she replied earnestly.

"Uh, yes. Of course. But still…" The guy was having a really hard time finishing any thoughts. Finally, he settled on, "And who's this lucky fellow with you, Miss Mendez?"

"This is my good friend, Jim Kelley," she replied.

Chet turned and engaged in the usual politician's fist-pumping handshake. She listened on as Jim wished the senator luck in the upcoming election. But Chandler's gaze kept straying back to her and then shifting back and forth between her and Jim. It was clear that Chet thought Jim was dating his junior aide with an eye to getting access to the senator himself. Such hubris the man had. But then, he was an elected official. She supposed it came with the territory.

As Jim was turning away from Chandler, a snippet of murmured conversation floated back to the micro-hearing aid in her right ear. Jim wasn't wearing one because of his short hair, but the device was hidden just fine under her long tresses.

She recognized Chandler's voice. "Who's the guy with Alex? And why's he with my staffer? Obviously, he wants something, but what?"

If Jim wanted to kick the hornet's nest and stir up a reaction, it appeared his tactic was working. She was surprised, though, when Jim suggested not much later that the two of them leave the party.

"You paid a lot of money to be here. Are you sure you want to go?" she responded in surprise.

He grinned down at her. "Any guy out with a woman as beautiful as you would seem strange if he didn't want to leave early and have her all to himself somewhere more private." He added, "I'm just playing out our cover."

Right. Then why did her stomach flutter wildly at the idea of him having her all to himself in private? Her brain might be able to distinguish between work and play, cover story and reality, but her body was having no part of it. Languor stole through her bones at the mere thought of being alone with Jim.

With jovial farewells from several of the McNaught representatives, Jim rested his hand on her waist and guided her out. Lord, her pulse jumped around like popcorn in hot oil when he touched her like that. Heat radiated outward from his palm, engulfing her entire body.

Jim tensed beside her but didn't remove his hand. His BMW was brought around, he handed her into it, and then he stomped on the accelerator as they peeled out of the hotel.

"I know it's a high-performance car," she announced. "You don't have to demonstrate it on my account."

"All part of the cover," he replied, grinning. "I'm a risk-taker, remember?"

"You've always been a risk-taker. You don't have to pretend on that score."

He glanced over at her, his smile turning painful. "You know me too well."

Right now she didn't know him nearly well enough. What was he thinking after their sexy charade tonight? She felt as if her brain had been thrown in a blender and tossed around until she had no idea what to think or feel.

She steered the conversation toward safer, work-related ground. "The gang at the fundraiser was definitely curious about you. I heard Chet Chandler tell one of the bigwigs from McNaught to find out what you want from him. Apparently, the only reason a guy like you would move in on a girl like me is to get to him."

"Is Chandler *blind?*" Jim exclaimed. "All anyone has to do is take one look at you to know why a guy like me would date a woman like you."

Alex subsided. He'd called her a woman. That was a first. And she had to admit, she liked it. Enough to think about going out with Carla and getting some more girly clothes and maybe even doing the hair and makeup thing again. Although the whole idea of primping on a regular basis felt bizarre. As much as she might pine over her lost femininity, the fact remained that she'd never actually been a makeup-and-frilly-clothes kind of gal to begin with. She'd been too young to know if those things would interest her when she'd cut them out of her life.

She was shocked when they arrived at the apartment building on Capitol Hill that Jim only pulled up to the curb and kept the Beemer idling. "You're not coming up?" she asked.

"Can't," he mumbled. "Work. Gotta check in with Delta Company. I'll call you tomorrow." And with that, he all but kicked her out of the car.

Whoa. She hadn't seen that one coming. The old hurt rolled through her, newer and more miserable than ever. Who in the heck was she trying to kid? How'd that saying go? You could give a sow a silk purse, but she'd still be a pig? Apparently you could dress up a Mendez like a girl, but she was still one of the guys at the end of the day.

Of course, Jim's attraction to her had all been an act. A cover. What had she been thinking? She'd let her stupid fantasies run away with her. She'd completely imagined that heat smoking in his eyes every time he'd looked at her. God, how desperate and pathetic was that?

Stunned and more than a little humiliated, she stumbled up to the love nest alone. A sick certainty settled in her gut that she was forever doomed to be just one of the guys. All of her secret dreams to be loved and cherished as a woman were just that. Dreams.

Frustrated beyond all reason, she kicked off her shoes, stripped off her dress, and flopped across the big bed. Things were back to ops normal, apparently. Jim didn't want a thing to do with her, and she got to toss and turn for hours wishing for something that would never be between them. Except now she knew what it felt like to be held in his arms. And that made it a million times worse.

Jim tossed and turned in his bed, unaccustomed to the frustration raging through him. Normally, when he was this attracted to a woman, he brought her home with him and scratched the itch. But God almighty, this was Alex he was lusting after! What in the hell was he supposed to do about that?

And what about the McNaught Group? Had he made enough of an impression on them for someone to contact him? The senior partners had played their cards very close to the chest. Definitely some secrets hiding behind that slick corporate facade.

What did power brokers like them want with his father? What had Hank brought to the table that McNaught needed? Was it as simple as controlling votes in Congress? Hank had served on the powerful House Appropriations Committee. Was that why McNaught wanted to own him? Or was it something more sinister, like wanting to use the Kelley clan's long association with the Colton family, and more specifically, Joe Colton, President of the United States? Surely McNaught wouldn't reach that high. But Jim fell asleep wondering about it.

No surprise, he dreamed about the accident. Except this

time it was Alex crashing through the windshield in a spray of glass and blood.

It was nearly 5:00 a.m. when his phone rang. He woke with a jolt, swearing at the nightmare. "Kelley, here," he mumbled into the receiver.

"Hey, it's me."

Jim sat up abruptly. His boss Austin Kittredge from Homeland Security. The man who'd brought him in on the investigation into Lana's kidnapping…and the larger investigation of the Raven's Head Society behind it. "What's up?"

"We just got an alert that your bank records and stockbrokerage account were hacked into a few minutes ago."

Jim frowned. "What did the hacker do to my assets?"

"Nothing," Kittredge replied. "Apparently, he was just looking."

Outstanding. He and Alex had Lana's kidnappers rattled. His hunter's instincts sharpened at the scent of his prey. He'd take the bastards down if it was the last thing he did. No one messed with his family.

"Wow. The hornets didn't take long to strike."

"Come again?" Kittredge responded.

"I kicked a hornet's nest last night. Bunch called the Mc-Naught Group. When Mendez was taking her extracurricular peek into Chandler's computer, she took a look at Chandler's campaign donors. Turns out a lot of them have ties to this McNaught crew. We researched them and found out the same cluster of donors contributed to my father's last campaign."

"Interesting."

"The McNaught Group sponsored a fundraiser for Senator Chandler last night and I was able to get Alex and me lastminute tickets." He added with a wince, "There's going to be a sixty-thousand-dollar charge on the credit card you issued me for this op to cover the dinner."

Austin whistled. "In case you haven't heard, the government's got a small deficit problem. Could you try not to add too much to it, buddy?"

"Trust me. The food wasn't worth half that. But I did make some fascinating contacts. The key players at McNaught seemed to know exactly who I was. A few of them asked me obliquely if I have the ear of my family's old friend, Joe Colton."

Kittredge replied soberly, "Sounds like cash well spent, then." He added more lightly, "It's nice when an operative comes to me with his own financial cover portfolio."

Jim frowned. "Speaking of that, I could use a dummy bank account offshore while Homeland Security is artificially enhancing my portfolio."

"But we already added enough zeroes to your accounts to make you nearly a billionaire," Kittredge exclaimed.

"These McNaught guys play outside the rules. I'm going to have to demonstrate my willingness to screw the government to get them to consider playing ball with me."

"How much do you want and where?" Kittredge asked.

Jim breathed a sigh of relief. His boss was going to play ball. "Something in the Caymans to the tune of a billion dollars or so."

"Seriously?"

"Yeah."

"Okay, Jim. You've got it. Just remember, it won't be real money, though. Don't try to spend any of it."

He laughed. "Got it. I'll try not to buy any multinational corporations with it. Although I promise I'd make you a ton of money if I did a deal like that for you."

"Just remember that, unlike you, my office has a tight budget. Don't kill me with your expense account, eh?"

"If I can nail Lana's kidnappers, I'll pay for the whole damned thing out of my own pocket," Jim retorted.

"Can I quote you on that?"

"How long will it take to set up the Cayman account?" Jim retorted.

"About an hour after the office opens this morning. I'll call my resident computer expert and have her get right on it."

"Mendez?" Jim blurted.

"You know anyone better than her?" Kittredge replied.

"Nah. She's the best. And by the way, you ought to see her in a dress. She looked like a freaking movie star at the fundraiser."

"No way," Kittredge declared.

"Hack the security cameras from the McNaught fundraiser at the Baywater Hotel last night. She's the ravishing brunette I brought as my date."

"This I have to see."

"Just don't tell her I had anything to do with you getting pictures. She'd kill me."

His boss laughed. "She can be a bit prickly, can't she?"

"Just a bit."

Jim was wide awake after the call. Rather than lie in bed stewing, he got up and went down to the state-of-the-art gym in his basement to work out. It was disconcerting how often as he sweated that his thoughts strayed to stunning brunettes in sexy red dresses. And she thought he had a thing for blondes. Hah!

His day was mostly taken up with paperwork. Even clandestine units like his had administrative necessities. The clock on his desk seemed to crawl, as though taunting him over his impatience to head over to the love nest after work. He kept telling himself he was just curious to see what Alex had learned today and to find out if there'd been any fallout from Chandler seeing her at the fundraiser. But even he didn't believe it.

The drive across Washington at rush hour just about did

in his nerves. It took him nearly two hours to get from his office in suburban Virginia to Capitol Hill. But finally, he turned into the parking garage. He pulled in beside the Beast, smiling at her junker. The car was a lot like her. Not much to look at on the outside, but rock-solid beneath. He glanced at the Beast as he got out of his car. He suspected that with a little body work and a good wax job the Beast would clean up into a half-decent classic car. Kind of like its owner.

He was curious to see which Alex would be waiting for him today—the wannabe combat technician or the sultry sex kitten.

He let himself into the apartment and was stunned when a fast-moving, dark-haired projectile immediately launched herself at him. He caught Alex's lithe body up against his in reflex and was further stunned when she plastered her mouth to his.

Holy crap. Kissing Arturo's little sister. Bad. Very bad. Like kissing his little brother except she tasted like vanilla Chapstick. But holy cow, could she kiss!

The sizzle between them was instantaneous and incendiary. Her mouth softened and opened beneath his and her body turned to liquid silk in his arms, and suddenly, he needed no encouragement to kiss her back. She was all woman and any thought of other things flew right out of his head.

She moaned in the back of her throat and a need to inhale the provocative sound overwhelmed him. Her hands came up to cup either side of his face, and he angled his head to kiss her more deeply as her fingertips urged him on.

Her tongue touched his, and the kiss leaped to an entirely new level of intensity as he swept his tongue inside her mouth, demanding more from her and taking everything she gave in return. He kicked the door shut with his foot and took several steps into the living room with her, his hands roaming up and down her spine, savoring the sweet give of her curves beneath his palms.

The couch was only a few more steps away. He had a vague idea of carrying her down to it. Getting her out of her clothes. Kissing her entire body from brows to toes. Exploring just how much of a tiger the kitten had turned into.

She tugged his head down and kissed her way up his jaw to nibble his earlobe. But then she breathed against his ear, "Audio bugs in here and the bedroom. No cameras." She moaned audibly and announced, "Do that again."

He stared down at her in dismay. McNaught had already found and bugged this place? Man, they were *good.* An old football buddy of his owned this condo, and Alex had no connection to the owner whatsoever.

He groaned back for the benefit of the bugs, "God, you're hot."

Her eyebrows shot up as he led her by the hand into the bedroom. He plunked down on the side of the bed and gestured for her to do the same. The mattress gave a satisfying creak. Perfect. Grinning, he pushed her down onto her back and rolled onto his side, supporting himself over her on one elbow. He unzipped her jeans and she gasped as the teeth made a metallic zinging noise.

"Mmm," he sighed as he leaned down to kiss her neck, smacking his lips loudly.

She startled him by reaching for his trousers and pulling down his zipper, too. Her hands were small and warm against his belly and his body reacted powerfully to her touch.

He swore, and she laughed.

"Vixen," he muttered. He slid his free hand under the edge of her T-shirt, running his palm over the indent of her waist and higher, along her ribs. She arched away from the invasion, but that forced her to roll into him, her breasts coming into impudent contact with his chest. He grinned down at her.

"Oh, baby," he groaned.

Her brother's dark eyes gazed up at him and he jolted. Did she have to look so damned much like Arturo? She startled him by groaning back, "Oh, yes. Right there."

The raw lust in her voice made his gut tighten until it hurt. *Wench.* He retorted, "That's it. Open for me. Oh, yes. Give it to me. I want all of you."

Her eyes registered surprise. She moaned back, "Take me, Jim. I'm yours. Anything you want. Oh…" Her voice rose on a little scream. "Yes! Yes!"

He bounced up and down on the mattress beside her and she got into the spirit of the thing immediately, bouncing in rhythm beside him.

They groaned and moaned for several minutes, with Alex credibly faking no less than three orgasms. Inspired, he commenced rocking back and forth hard enough to bang the headboard into the wall.

He rocked and she bounced faster and faster, until finally she shouted, "Oh, baby. Give it to me hard! Yes, yes, yes!" She then keened in what could only be the mother of all multiple orgasms before finally collapsing back against the mattress, panting audibly. She grinned triumphantly at him.

Silent laughter shook him, and he fell to his back beside her.

She commented breathlessly, "Don't worry about it. You'll last longer next time."

He popped up to his elbow to stare down at her in disbelief. "Four orgasms weren't good enough for you? Good Lord, woman, you're going to kill me."

"That's the idea," she purred back at him.

Apparently, the absurdity of it all overcame her then because she clapped a hand over her mouth to stifle her laughter. Her eyes sparkled like black diamonds. *Ahh, God…Arty.* How he missed his friend. The two of them had been born on the same day and had been like a pair of inseparable puppies, tumbling through his childhood summers in Montana, fighting and scrapping and defending each other from all comers. They'd been seventeen when the accident cut Arturo's life all too short.

He shook his head and grinned down at Alex. "How about a shower with me? I'll see if I can do better in there."

"Mmm, sounds fun," she sighed. "Last one in the shower's a rotten egg."

He retorted, "Last one in the shower gets the cold tiles of the wall."

She bounded out of bed, laughing. He followed her into the bathroom and closed the door while she turned on the cold water full-blast. She sat down on the closed toilet-seat lid and he perched on the edge of the oversized soaker tub.

Under the cover of the noisy spray, he asked, "What's up with the bugs?"

She shrugged. "When I got home from work, I did a routine electronic sweep and picked up a field that wasn't there this morning. I searched the place and found two bugs. One in the lamp beside the bed and one behind an electrical outlet in the living room. Professional job."

"And you're sure there are no more bugs? No cameras?"

"None. I did a thorough electronic sweep of the place followed by a detailed physical search. We're not on *Candid Camera*. At least not yet."

He grinned. "After our performance out there, they may just put cameras in the place to catch the show."

She grinned back at him.

"Did Kittredge get a hold of you this morning?" he asked.

Her smile faded. "Yes. And you're now officially a billionaire. As if you needed to be wealthier than you already are."

He nodded grimly. "Any hits on the Caymans account yet?"

"Not yet. It may take them a couple of days to find it. I hid the account pretty well."

He frowned. "But we want them to find it."

"They'd get suspicious if they found your offshore money too easily," she replied.

"Good point. Any reaction from Chandler today?"

She rolled her eyes. "Yeah. He sent a memo out to all his female staffers saying that with an election coming up he expects frequent media visitors to the office and we should all wear makeup and flattering fashions that will look good on camera."

"Wow. Really subtle," Jim commented.

She shrugged. "Apparently, he thinks having a hot babe in the office will help his image."

"At least with male voters it will."

She stuck her tongue out at him, then stood up, cracked open the bathroom door and startled him by shrieking, "Whoo, baby!"

As she closed the door he remarked wryly, "This op will do wonders for my reputation as an epic stud."

"Like you didn't already have that rep?" she mumbled.

He wasn't sure he was supposed to hear the comment, and he had no idea how to respond to it. He wasn't about to admit that when Alex had been moaning and groaning before, he'd wished that he was actually driving her out of her mind with pleasure. Personally, he hadn't been faking his groans, although they'd been born of frustration rather than satisfied lust. Far from satisfied lust, in fact.

She turned off the water and they waited a few more minutes to account for drying off before they stepped out into the bedroom.

"I don't know about you, Jim, but I'm going to have to eat before I do that again tonight."

He rolled his eyes. "Me, too. I've worked up a bit of an appetite. Do you want to eat in or go out?"

"I like eating naked. There's so much you can do with food, you know."

Images of her breasts wreathed in whipped cream, her luscious stomach drizzled in chocolate sauce flashed through his head. His sexual frustration climbed yet another notch. "Eating in it is," he replied. He added slyly, "And I know exactly what I'm having for dessert."

Alex's gaze snapped to his, and her breath hitched satisfyingly.

They talked about inconsequential things over dinner—the latest movies, their favorite music, the day's news headlines. He'd never doubted she was intelligent, but he hadn't been aware how wide-ranging her interests were. How could she work for him for a year and he know so little about her? With any other guy in his unit, he could rattle off even the smallest details of their lives and interests. It was his job to know his men that well. It allowed him to match up exactly the right operator with each mission that came along.

But here was Alex, speaking about literature with as much ease as she talked about world affairs or sports, and he'd had no idea she cared about any one of the three until tonight. He had to admit it was refreshing being around a woman who wasn't afraid to use her brains openly in front of him. Although, it did beg the question of whether the women he'd dated in the past had hidden their intelligence from him or not had any to hide at all.

Alex wasn't entirely wrong when she'd accused him of having a propensity for beautiful blondes. He was sure there were plenty of brilliant blondes in the world, but he suspected he'd never asked any of them out. He really had been all about appearances in the past.

An alarming thought struck him. Alex didn't think he was

suddenly interested in her purely because of her changed looks, did she? Aloud, he said, "You know, I enjoy talking with you. You're an interesting person."

"Hah," she retorted, "you're just desperate to distract me so you can recover before I take you back to bed and have my indecent way with you."

Indecent? He could think of a few indecent things he'd love to do with her. His gaze narrowed. "Don't tempt me. I don't want you so sore tomorrow that you can't walk."

Her gaze widened. Imagining what he had in mind, was she? Good. Misery loved company.

Alex was stunned. She would never in her wildest dreams have guessed that Jim would show this flirtatious and frankly sexual side of himself to her. Even if they were putting on a show for the people at the other end of the bugs, he was going way beyond the call of duty. Did she dare hope it was because he actually had thoughts along those lines where she was concerned?

When she'd been moaning and groaning earlier, it had been shockingly easy to tap into her fantasies of him and imagine how he would make her feel if they'd actually been making love. She probably wouldn't be quite so loud about it given her druthers, but the intensity of her response to him was entirely realistic if she had to guess.

She studied him over a slice of Chicago-style deep-dish pizza. The boy she'd followed around obsessively, and the teen she'd later mooned over endlessly, had become a man. A self-possessed, sexually confident man who was as sure of himself in bed as he was about everything else he did. If she'd been attracted to him before, she was doubly so after their little performance earlier. She supposed the idea of being listened to in bed ought to put a damper on her lust, but it didn't do a blessed thing to deter entirely inappropriate thoughts of taking him back to the bedroom, stripping him down and doing for real all of the things they'd faked before.

Girly girls probably didn't ravish their men, though. They probably let the man take the lead and just hoped the guy happened to be a considerate enough lover to give them some pleasure along the way. She wasn't all that experienced with sex herself. The few guys she'd actually slept with had seemed intimidated when she'd told them forthrightly what she liked and wanted.

The last one had accused her of wanting to wear the pants in the relationship and had bailed on her after one lousy night together. It still hurt that she was so inadequate as a woman in that department. But then, she was generally inadequate in most female departments.

Jim waved her back down to the couch when she would have stood up to throw away their paper plates, and he cleaned up the remnants of their meal himself. But when he returned from the kitchen, he shocked her by drawing her to her feet and into his arms.

"I've had a nice evening," he murmured quietly enough that it was clear he was talking directly to her and not for the benefit of the bug in the room. "Thank you."

As she stared in open shock, he leaned down and kissed her. Just a light brush of his lips against hers, warm and gentle and undemanding. He released her and stepped back with a faint smile. But ohmigosh. He'd kissed her. Really kissed her...not for an audience, but just between the two of them. She was still staring as he let himself out of the apartment and the door closed quietly behind him.

Chapter 6

A fascinating message was waiting for Jim on his answering machine when he got home. "Hi, Jim. This is Roscoe Harrington. We met at the Chandler fundraiser last night. I was wondering if you'd like to get together at my club for lunch tomorrow...."

Bingo. Harrington was a McNaught man, and a senior one if he'd correctly read the body language of the other McNaught men around him last night.

He returned Roscoe's call and got the man's voice mail. He left a brief message accepting the date and hung up. Taking advantage of the secure phone line and white-noise machine Alex had installed in his townhouse several months ago at the request of Kittredge, Jim picked up the phone again and dialed his sister, Lana.

"Hey, big brother," she answered. "How are you doing?"

He winced. Ever since the kidnapping, a certain joy had gone out of his sister. She was a fighter and had given the kidnappers as good as they got from her, but it had taken a toll on her. Renewed determination to find and punish whoever'd messed with her coursed through him. "I'm great, little sis. You? Ready to pop the kid yet?"

She laughed. "I've still got a few more months to go. The baby's kicking a lot now. It's pretty cool."

She sounded a little more like her old self as she talked about the baby. Deacon, God bless him, had gotten Lana away from the kidnappers before they succeeded in breaking her. With time and his love, she would heal.

Lana was speaking again. "...Deacon can't keep his hands off my baby bump."

A brief image of his baby growing inside a golden-skinned belly flashed through Jim's head. Whoa. He and Alex weren't even dating officially. He was getting way ahead of himself, here.

"What's up with calling me this late?" Lana was asking.

"I was wondering if Deacon ever heard any of the men in the Raven's Head Society mention a company called the Mc-Naught Group or a guy named Roscoe Harrington."

"Just a sec. I'll ask him."

A male voice came on the line moments later. "Hey, Jim. What's up?"

"I think I may have found how the Raven's Head Society moves around its financial resources. A bunch of the guys we think are involved with them are senior executives or board members of a company called the McNaught Group."

"I've never heard the name, but I saw a couple of memos referring to M.G. when financial transactions came up."

Jim nodded. He and Alex were definitely on the right track, then. "Any idea what these guys might be up to?"

"Yeah. Lana and I have been comparing notes about stuff we overheard. We think they had a specific plan in mind when they recruited Hank. They wanted him to participate in something."

"Like what?"

"We don't know. But it was secret. And if Hank or any of the other participants got caught, they'd have gone to jail or worse."

"So it was something illegal?" Jim asked.

"Very illegal. Dangerous. Maybe violent."

That gave Jim pause. What on earth had Hank gotten himself tangled up in? His father might be a philanderer and a liar, but he wasn't the kind of man who intentionally hurt other people.

"Anything else?" Jim asked.

"Not so far. We'll let you know if we come up with more."

"Take care of Lana and the baby, eh?"

"Count on it," Deacon replied grimly.

Jim stared at the phone thoughtfully after he hung up. What in the hell were McNaught and the secret society hiding behind it up to? He was startled out of his thoughts by his cell phone beeping with an incoming text.

The number was Alex's. Calling for some phone sex, now, was she? Grinning, he opened the message.

Guess who I just linked to McNaught.

Damn. Not phone sex. He texted back a question mark.

I had to dig deep, but...Victor Metzger.

The Vice President of the United States? Jim had heard rumors about the man but discounted them as impossible. If Metzger was in the McNaught Group's pocket, though, that gave the rumors a whole lot more weight. The horrifying possibilities of corruption in the White House made his temples throb with the beginnings of a headache.

His response to Alex said it all.

Keep digging.

It felt weird in the morning to put her hair up in hot rollers and paint on makeup while they cooled. She pulled out the narrow skirt that had garnered all the cat calls at Jim's unit a few days ago and paired it with one of her white Oxford shirts. But she wore the lace-edged camisole under it that Carla had insisted she buy, and she left a few more buttons undone than usual. She brushed out her hair, sprayed it a little to hold the curls, and stood back to survey the results.

Seriously, she hardly recognized the woman in the mirror. Now, how to arrange to see Jim today? After all, there was no sense wasting a good outfit and girly primping, was there?

She was startled by the intensity of the reaction of the front-desk guards at the Dirksen Building. They stared at her as though an alien had possessed her. Staffers up and down the hallways all but fell over themselves double-taking on her, and Trevor McKinley nearly killed himself choking on a bagel when she stepped into Chandler's office.

And then there was the steady stream of aides who made excuses to visit Chandler's office through the morning. It was downright embarrassing. Enough to drive her out for lunch to escape the stares and whispers. It was a crisp day with brilliant blue skies and leaves scuffing under foot. She walked toward the Mall, enjoying the scores of people lounging on the grass, a microcosm of America.

It was probably because she was actively looking around at the families and tourists that she noticed the man trailing far behind her. He was very good, actually. But then, so was she. She didn't change her stride and continued people-watching as casually as before. But out of the corner of her eye she caught the hand-off as the first man peeled away after a few blocks and another one took up the tail. This man moved in a bit closer to her.

Who were they? McNaught men? Were they dangerous or just curious?

A woman took the hand-off from the second man, and she closed to within a block of Alex. Three people tailing her? Disquiet rumbled in her gut. That was a whole lot of resources for one insignificant girlfriend of someone who wasn't even an investor in their company.

When a third man took over from the woman—who made a point of pulling ahead of Alex on the other side of the street—and the first man appeared at her flank on the grass of the Mall, Alex's disquiet erupted into full-blown alarm. She was being encircled. But for what purpose? Her operational security training said they were positioning themselves for one maneuver and one maneuver only. A grab-and-go kidnapping. Any minute a car or a van would pull up to the curb out of nowhere and she'd be toast. She pulled out her cell phone and dialed Jim's number.

"Kelley, here," he answered briskly.

He must not be alone. "Can you talk?" she asked as she walked.

"Nope. You?"

"I'm being followed by at least three men and a woman who are encircling me as we speak. Is it possible they plan to snatch me to put some sort of pressure on you?"

"Makes sense. I'm at the Young Republican Club for lunch. I can drive by there in a little while, or you can meet me somewhere else."

She thought fast. The Young Republican Club was in northwest D.C. But a Metro stop was a block ahead of her current position. "I'm coming to you. I'm scared."

"Sounds good. I'll see you then."

She put away her phone and ducked down the Metro steps. As soon as she was below street level, she took off in a full-out sprint. She slammed her Metro card through the reader and took off running the second the machine spat it out.

She dived into the first stairwell, which didn't go to the train she needed. But she heard the rumble of a train coming and raced for the platform. The doors were just closing as she got there and she leaped onto the train at the last possible second. She crouched between two rows of plastic seats and refrained from lifting her head to peek outside as the train pulled out of the station. If her pursuers were out there, the last thing she wanted to do was give them a chance to spot her and give chase.

Thankfully, she saw the train was mostly empty. She made a production of pretending to find something on the floor and then took a seat as darkness closed in around the train.

She got off several stops later and repeated the maneuver, sprinting for a random train as it approached. After three transfers with no sign of a tail, she actually headed for a train that would take her to Jim.

Why on earth would the McNaught Group be interested in her? Surely, they hadn't traced her internet IP and realized she was the person who'd been researching them and their various corporations. She'd been using rotating servers and a dummy address. Even if they had figured out who she was, didn't it make sense that she was researching them on behalf of her supposed boyfriend? All the information she'd been looking at had been public. She shouldn't have set off any alarms.

But, apparently, she had. Or maybe it was the coincidence of Chandler's staffer showing up with some rich guy who was showing an interest in McNaught that caused the flap. But either way, that team had definitely been closing in on her. She was not being paranoid.

She pulled her hair back into a ponytail and searched her bag for a scarf or something to cover her white shirt. Nada. She would have to start carrying a wig and a spare blouse in her purse, apparently. She ducked into a souvenir shop as soon as she exited the Metro and bought a black, I ♥ DC T-shirt, sunglasses, a pair of cheap sandals, and a big straw bag. She slipped into the tiny storeroom in back to change and stuffed her purse, white Oxford blouse and shoes into the large bag. She stepped out onto the street, using the cover of her sunglasses to hide her careful search of the pedestrians nearby. Nobody looked like her followers from before. Either she'd lost them or they'd switched to a completely new team with under a half hour's notice. In which case, the McNaught Group was too darned good for her.

She walked rapidly toward the Young Republican Club and no one kept pace with her. As best she could tell, she was clean. She circled around behind the club and headed for the parking lot. She spied Jim's BMW and prayed he'd unlocked it with his keyless remote.

During their brief conversation he'd made a point of mentioning that he'd drive somewhere to meet her, indicating that he had his car with him. She hoped she'd interpreted his meaning correctly. She ducked down between the parked rows of cars and crept awkwardly toward his car. She tried one of the back doors and found blessedly that it was open. She slipped inside and lay down on the leather seat. She locked the doors, then pulled out her cell phone. Undoubtedly, Jim's phone was set to vibrate only during his meeting. She dialed it, let it ring once and hung up.

She didn't have to wait long. In under ten minutes, Jim unlocked his door, slid behind the wheel and guided the car out of the parking lot without once speaking to her or in any way indicating that she was lying in his back seat. After about five minutes of driving he finally announced, "We're clear. You can sit up. What the hell's going on, Alex?"

"I was hoping you could tell me," she retorted without sitting up.

"I just had lunch with a heavy-hitter from McNaught. By rights, I should have passed through several layers of junior nobodies before I got to a guy like him. He wants me to send him my complete financial records to see if I meet their criteria for becoming an investor with them."

"That's good, right?" she asked.

"We've definitely got their attention," he agreed. "More significantly, he was very interested in my father's medical condition and whether he's expected to recover from his coma any time soon. I lied. Told him the prognosis is not good and that we're basically waiting for him to die."

"How'd he react to that?"

"He relaxed, of all things."

"That's weird."

Jim continued, "And then he started asking me about what will happen to my father's investments and who will take over my father's seat in Congress when he dies. He intimated that I might be a good choice to step in and serve out my father's term until the next election. He even probed to see if I have an interest in pursuing politics in the long term."

"Do you?" she asked, startled.

"Hell, no. Too many reporters would poke into my past. Someone would find out who I've worked with for all these years."

"Yeah, the United States Army is a pretty dodgy outfit."

He snorted. "They've made a good cover story for my real job."

She turned that comment over in her head. She'd had to obtain outrageously high-level security clearances before she'd been loaned to Jim's unit, supposedly an army team stationed in Washington, D.C., to supplement various security details for government officials. But the teams spent an inordinate amount of time away from the office at "training" or on seemingly simple missions that didn't require nearly the manpower that had been assigned to them. And she'd been tasked to provide some pretty exotic gear to the teams during the time she'd been supporting them. Before she'd been assigned to her backwater desk job on Chandler's staff, that was.

"What exactly does your unit do, anyway?" she demanded.

"You know the mission. Provide supplemental security for important government assets."

"Who do you and I really work for?" she asked astutely.

Jim's answer was low. Grim. "Takes most guys a while to get around to that question. Better that you don't know the answer in case you're ever captured and questioned. They're the good guys, though."

"I'd have to go out into the field on an actual combat mission to come into any danger of being captured," she snapped.

He sighed. "We compartmentalize the unit as much as we possibly can. Information is briefed on specific missions on need-to-know basis only. And right now, you and I have our hands plenty full with this mission."

"Where are we going?" she asked next.

"I got an idea while I was with the McNaught guy."

She was silent for a while, turning over what he'd said. Then she piped up, "If our destination has access to the internet, I'd like to set up some additional security protocols to prevent my work from being traced."

"You think that's why the goon squad came after you?"

"Do you have any better ideas?" she challenged.

He drove in silence after that. She was uncomfortable lying in the backseat with a seat belt poking her hip, the seat hump in her side, and not quite enough room for her legs any-where. But it was a whole lot better than being spotted and chased again.

Jim drove for about twenty minutes. The car turned onto progressively quieter streets, and finally crunched onto what sounded like a driveway. Shortly thereafter, the car stopped. "We're here," he announced. "You really can unfold back there."

She sat up in relief. *Here* was the circular drive in front of an imposing Georgian brick estate with a stern facade. "Whose place is this?" she asked as she climbed out of the car and worked the kinks out of various muscles.

"It's my father's house."

Ahh. Good idea. They could check his computer files and see what dirt he might have left behind on the Raven's Head Society and McNaught. "How are we getting in?" she asked.

He grinned. "Spare key, of course."

He dangled a key chain and she sighed, declaring, "Still no real action in sight."

"What the hell do you call being chased and nearly kid-napped?" he demanded. "You had my adrenaline going plenty hard."

She frowned. "Why? You've been a field operative for-ever. Aren't you supposed to have nerves of steel?"

"Apparently not where my cute girl troops are concerned."

She knew he meant the comment harmlessly, but it bugged her a little that suddenly he was all concerned about her now that he thought she was cute. Surely, he cared about her for more than just her looks. Although the big one-eighty in his attitude had come the night he saw her in a sexy dress with her hair and makeup done to the nines.

"You coming or not?" he called from the front porch.

Sheesh. She'd been standing in the driveway like a zombie. She moved to join him as he let himself into the house. Predictably, the interior was as formal and intimidating as the outside. Definitely not a friendly place. It seemed more about projecting power and status than anything else.

"You like the ol' mausoleum?" Jim muttered.

"Not particularly," she replied under her breath. The house was so big and empty and echoing that it reminded her of a museum. It was the kind of place a person whispered in. "Did you grow up here?" she asked.

"Heck no. This is just my dad's Washington place. Mom kept us at home in California—that's Hank's official residence—where we could have at least a semblance of normalcy. And of course, we spent summers in Montana."

Summers that she had anticipated all year long and savored the memory of in vivid detail from September to May.

"Hank's office is this way." Jim led her down a hall that opened to the left. Strange how often he called his father by his first name. She would never dream of calling her father anything other than Pop. But then, Hank Kelley had never been that close to any of his kids. And once he got into politics he'd been gone most of the time.

She followed Jim into a predictably wood-paneled, leather-booked, giant-desked office that had the same grandeur as Hank Kelley. Jim sat down at the desk and booted up his father's computer while she did a lap around the office, admiring the Remington bronze statue of a bucking bronco, and checked out the amply stocked bar.

Jim swore quietly and she whirled in concern. "All the files have been deleted," he announced in disgust. "We're too late. These guys are really starting to piss me off."

She moved over to his side. "Maybe not." She opened the cabinet in the desk that contained the computer tower. "Have you got a screwdriver?"

Jim pulled out a pocket knife and used it to unscrew the computer case for her. She reached in carefully and unplugged the entire hard drive from the motherboard. She undid the last few fasteners and lifted the drive out of the system.

"When we get this back to the love nest, I've got a gizmo that can recover deleted files."

"I thought deleted files were, well, deleted," he responded.

She shook her head. "Nope. Every file leaves a permanent impression on the actual drive itself. Using computer forensic technology, I can recover all of it. It takes the right equipment and know-how, but before we're done, we'll know every dirty little secret that was ever stored on this puppy."

Jim shook his head. "Sometimes you're scary, Men—" He corrected himself. "—Alex."

Now why did he do that? In a work environment, he still thought of her by her last name. She was the scary techie he worked with. Why the correction to her first name? Was it because she was wearing makeup and a skirt again?

They searched the rest of the office, but eventually Jim announced, "There's nothing here."

"I imagined he kept—keeps—his important files in his office on Capitol Hill," she replied.

Jim threw her a grim look. "If this computer's been hacked and the files erased, I'd be dead certain everything regarding the Raven's Head Society or McNaught is long gone from there."

"I bet we get plenty off of this hard drive," she replied stoutly.

As they let themselves out of the house, she asked, "Is it safe to go back to the love nest?"

He replied deadpan, "I don't know if I can deliver a repeat performance of last night without keeling over."

She laughed in spite of her concerns. "You'd just better hope they haven't replaced those bugs with cameras, or then you'll really be in trouble."

His eyes flashed molten blue fire for a moment, but then he turned away, sliding behind the wheel of his car. The idea of doing for real what they'd faked last night made Alex flush from head to foot. The ride back to the love nest was uncomfortable and quiet. So much for the easy camaraderie of the past day. Her and her big mouth.

Chapter 7

Jim was having a hell of a time keeping his eyes on the road because his gaze kept straying over to Alex in the passenger seat beside him. Although the makeup was toned down and her hair was pulled back into a high, curly ponytail, her features were still the same as at the fundraiser. The wide, slightly tilted cat eyes. The great cheekbones and engaging smile. The lush, kissable lips. How was it he'd never seen all of that before?

Was it her fault for working so hard to blend in and be one of the guys? Or was it his fault for letting her? Either way, he'd been blind not to see it. And, frankly, he felt like a bit of an ass for having missed just how striking she was all this time.

Would he have treated her differently if he had noticed? His head said he'd have treated her just like all his other troops, as was appropriate and professional. But the twist in his gut every time he glanced over at her suggested otherwise.

Another woman in BDUs, a reasonably attractive and pleasant girl, flashed through his mind's eye.

With her face came memory of the constant taunts and jabs the other guys in the unit had thrown at her. The haunted look that had come into her eyes over time, the way she'd grown withdrawn and silent…God, he should've seen the signs. He'd been an idiot to let her sink or swim on her own. She'd been the first female tech assigned to his unit, and because he'd never had any big problem with the idea of women in the military, he'd mistakenly assumed that his troops wouldn't either. But he'd been wrong. *Dead* wrong. Had she not died on that first mission—he corrected himself—had she not committed suicide in the guise of being a hero, would he have been so slow to send Alex out?

Or would he have thrown her to the wolves, too? The thought of Alex tormented and hazed by his men made his gut clench unpleasantly. Arturo would've looked out for his little sis. He couldn't do any less for her in Arturo's place, could he?

Of course, this new surge of protectiveness had nothing to do with growling off any other males who had the temerity to notice how beautiful Alex really was. Right? Aww, hell. Who was he trying to kid?

What the hell was he thinking? He had no business getting territorial over her. She worked for him, for crying out loud. This op might call for them to pose as boyfriend and girlfriend, but the operative word there was *pose*.

That sizzling kiss she'd laid on him yesterday as he'd burst into the love nest flashed through his mind. He could definitely go for more of that with her. But what about her? What did she want? It wasn't as though he'd ever paid any attention to that before. He had no idea what kind of guys she dated or what made her laugh—other than bouncing on creaky beds and pretending to have epic sex.

"What do you like to do in your free time?" he asked without preamble.

She looked over at him, startled. "Why do you ask?"

"I just want to get to know you a little better."

"You've known me practically my whole life," she replied, shrugging. "You know as well as I do what I've always done with my free time."

Yeah, except he'd never paid attention before. How weird was this, knowing everything and nothing about her? He could name the first boy she'd ever dated, recite her worst and funniest experiences growing up, and yet he didn't know her hobbies or her favorite food, or even her favorite color. He might know stuff about her, but he didn't know the important stuff. As soon as they got a little down time he'd have to correct that.

He pulled into the love nest's garage and cut the engine. "Stay here," he announced. "I'll get the hard-drive reader and be back in a jiffy."

"Do you know what a hard-drive reader looks like?" she asked skeptically.

"Tell me."

"You couldn't tell a magnetic scanner from a cell-phone charger. I'm going with you."

"No!" he blurted. "It could be dangerous. If whoever's on the other end of those bugs hears me, they could send someone in to kill me."

She shrugged. "So I'll be quiet."

"This isn't a game, Alex."

"I'm well aware of that, Jim. I said I'll be quiet. But the truth is you have no idea what gear I need, and I can grab it in a few seconds and be out of there. I'm coming with you."

He huffed. Her logic was sound, dammit. But he didn't like the idea of putting her into danger. The intensity of his dislike for that concept startled him, in fact.

"I go first and you follow all my commands immediately and without question. Got it?" he snapped.

She smiled broadly. "Got it."

Gritting his teeth, he led her up the stairs to the third floor. He signaled her to proceed silently and she rolled her eyes. Then the minx signaled back that he should take the left-hand field of fire and she would cover the right.

He rolled his eyes back at her. She *so* wanted to do the whole commando thing, but he *so* wasn't letting that happen. He repeated his order to let him go in first. She subsided, looking surly. Tough.

He eased open the apartment door and sauntered inside casually. If cameras had been placed in here since they last checked for such devices, the two of them had to try to look marginally normal until they spotted the cameras.

Alex moved over to her gear in the corner and rummaged—impressively silently—through a box and came up with several pieces of equipment. Meanwhile, he moved back to the doorway, ostensibly fetching a jacket from the closet just inside the door, to listen for the elevators.

She continued to stuff gear into a canvas bag and moved on to closing and packing both of the laptops on the desk. He heard the telltale whir of an elevator coming. It could be just another resident coming home in the middle of the afternoon…or it could be someone coming to kill them.

He waved urgently at her and she glanced up. He signaled that they had to go. Now.

She nodded and jumped for the door. They slipped out and she raced down the hall as the elevator door dinged. As the whoosh of doors opening sounded behind him, he dove for the stairwell.

Alex was waiting, holding the door open for him. As he passed by her she shoved the door shut and then fiddled with the latch for a moment.

"I jammed it," she breathed.

He nodded and they tore down the stairs. He made Alex go first so he could use his body to shield her from bullets from above. Somewhere overhead the stairwell door rattled. Not an innocent neighbor coming home, then. Damn, these McNaught operatives were good.

Grimly, he pressed on, staying right on Alex's heels. They burst out into the parking garage and raced for his car. She threw the electronic gear in the back seat and dived in as he revved the motor. He burst out onto the street and it took every ounce of control he had to pull sedately out into traffic. But in urban settings, the best way to hide was to blend in. Squealing tires and careening around corners was the easiest way to get followed.

"Watch our six," he bit out as he navigated the crowded streets.

She nodded and turned around in the passenger seat, studying the cars behind them intently. Finally, after several tense minutes, she announced, "We're clear."

"We've got to get off the street," he replied tersely. He kept an eye out for the next parking garage and turned into the first one he spotted.

"Where is this?" Alex asked.

It happened to be a hotel. Perfect. "The Hays-Adam," he replied. "How do you feel about going camping for a day or two?"

"Just get me somewhere with electricity so I can read your father's hard drive."

A uniformed valet came up to his door and Jim climbed out of the car. He took one of the bags of computer gear from Alex while she took the other. He led her into an elevator that had her gaping at its opulence. Wait till she saw their room.

He checked in using a government credit card rather than one with his name on it. In a matter of minutes, he pushed open the door to their suite and stepped aside for Alex to enter.

She stopped just inside the door. "Seriously?"

"Like it?" he asked, amused.

"I don't know. It's a little rich for my blood."

He glanced around at the opulent elegance of the living room. "Give it a chance. It'll grow on you."

"That's the problem. Then I'll have to go back to my normal, drab life."

He laughed. "Nothing about you or your life is drab."

"How would you know?" she muttered under her breath.

She was right. But he planned to correct that as soon as possible. "Point taken," he replied quietly.

Her gaze jerked to his, surprised. An awkward silence threatened to build between them. Into it, he said briskly, "Let's do a quick electronic sweep as a matter of procedure."

She nodded and dug in her bag of magic toys. He helped her sweep both the living room and bedroom, and he took the bathroom while she searched the wet bar. They met in the living room.

"All clear," he reported.

"Ditto," she replied.

He grinned. "All right then, Einstein. Let's see what dear old Dad's hard drive can tell us."

She commandeered the desk and went to work, pulling out a power strip and plugging in an array of gadgets. She opened one of the laptops and hooked it into the spaghetti of cables and then carefully attached a series of wires to Hank's hard drive. She hit a button on the laptop and the whole mess came to life.

"How long's this going to take?" he asked.

"Several hours at a minimum. Depends on how much data is on the hard drive. If you want to go take a nap or something, feel free. I'll babysit this stuff."

"I'd rather stay with you if you don't mind," he replied.

That made her gaze snap to his again. He thought he glimpsed pleasure in her dark eyes before she masked it. That was reassuring at any rate. For as long as he could remember, he'd been vaguely aware that she was sweet on him. He'd hate to have ignored her for so long that she no longer gave a damn about him.

He pulled up an armchair and propped his feet on the coffee table she'd pulled over to hold her extra gear. "Any thoughts on what our next step should be?" he said.

"You're asking me?"

"Why do you sound so surprised?" he retorted.

"Since when do you care what I think?"

He frowned. "I've always cared what you think."

She laughed. "No, you haven't. You've ignored me my whole life."

"I have not." He felt weird denying it when he'd only seconds before had the exact same thought. But it was the chivalrous thing to do. He would never knowingly hurt Alex's feelings. Truth was, she was practically a Kelley, and it turned out his protective impulses extended to her, too.

"What universe have you been living in?" she demanded. "Of course you've ignored me."

He sighed. "I was just trying to treat you like everyone else in the unit. I didn't want to draw undue attention in your direction. You're the only girl tech we've got and you're really young to have been pulled onto our team."

"I'm twenty-four," she declared.

"Like I said. Young."

She scowled but didn't argue the point.

He gestured at the hard-drive reader. "How does that thing work?"

"It reads the actual magnetic charges on the surface of the hard drive. The ones and zeros. Then this cable carries the signals to my laptop, which is running a translation program to reconstruct the information into a form recognizable to humans, be it text or a visual image. It won't be as pretty as if we opened a word-processing program or photo viewer program, but we'll be able to see all the data."

"Cool." He paused and then added, "So, you dodged my question before. What do you like to do in your spare time these days?"

She frowned. "I don't have much spare time."

"Fine. What do you do when you're not at the unit doing your job or at Chandler's office doing your job there?"

"I study up on new technologies. Work on my computer to learn all I can. Take kickboxing lessons. Run. The usual stuff."

"None of that sounds very usual for an attractive single female in a hopping town like this. Do you go out? Have friends? Date?" He added that last question as casually as he could, but he feared his voice tightened up on the word. For some bizarre reason, the idea of other guys putting their hands on Alex made him tense and grouchy.

She sighed. "I never have been any good at all that social stuff. But you know that."

Did he know that? He thought back to summers when she'd been a teen. He didn't recall guys coming out to the ranch to hang around her the way they had with Lana. Mostly, he remembered her hanging out with her father, wearing a pair of denim overalls, her head stuck in some engine or gizmo in need of repair.

"How's your dad?" he asked.

"Good. I haven't talked to him in a while, though. I should call him."

"I always envied you your closeness with him," Jim admitted.

"Really? I always envied you your big, rich family."

He smiled, but little by way of humor made it into the expression. "It wasn't all it was cracked up to be."

"I dunno. You had a pretty cushy life. And you and your siblings were pretty close."

A pang shot through him. Something else to feel like a heel for. She'd missed out on that closeness with Arturo. She'd been not quite thirteen when he'd died. Arturo was just starting to see her as something other than a snot-nosed brat trailing along after him, being a nuisance. They'd never gotten to grow up together and find a mature family bond.

Belatedly, he mumbled, "My siblings and I had to be close. Hank was always gone pursuing his political career, and Mom was busy helping him and trying to keep his attention. We got left to our own devices a lot."

"You had everything you ever wanted. Cars, clothes, cool vacations, fancy private schools," she retorted.

He shrugged. "None of that compares to a parent who really loves you and is there for you." At least she'd had her dad. He recalled the two of them being inseparable through her teen years.

"The way I remember it, your parents loved all of you kids," she commented.

"In a distant way, maybe. But not fiercely and immediately like your dad loves you. Rikki would walk on broken glass for you."

She laughed. "And he'd dare the glass to mess with me while he was at it."

Maybe that was where some of her self-confidence came from. Lucky girl. He opened his mouth to say so, but the laptop beeped just then and Alex leaned forward intently.

"Something wrong?" he bit out.

"Nope. The first images are reconstructing."

Over the next several hours, a steady stream of text and the occasional picture flashed across Alex's computer screen. She sifted through the deluge of information, setting up search parameters and enlisting Jim's aid in developing a set of key words to search for within the storm of documents reconstructing on her computer.

And then they started getting hits in her search algorithm. A document from the McNaught group promising a hefty campaign contribution. Several emails from known McNaught executives. No doubt about it, Hank had been tangled up with the Raven's Head Society and McNaught was a front for the outfit. But what exactly was that bunch up to?

He ordered room service for supper—a tray of cold sandwiches and fruit they could snack on throughout the evening. Alex had just picked up a ham and swiss on rye when she slammed the sandwich down suddenly and smacked herself in the forehead with her palm.

"What?" he asked, alarmed.

"Encryption," she declared, disgusted, as she began to type rapidly.

What in the heck was she talking about? "Come again?"

"Encryption. I didn't tell my system to look for encrypted documents. And surely anything of importance pertaining to the Raven's Head Society would be encrypted. I'm such an idiot!"

She was anything but an idiot. However, he didn't interrupt her intense concentration to correct her. In a matter of seconds, random letters and numbers started scrolling down her screen. "Bingo," she exclaimed.

"You're happy about random gobbledygook?" he asked.

She grinned at him. "Watch this." She typed in a series of commands to her computer and then sat back. In a few seconds, the random symbols began resolving themselves into words, and then sentences, and then paragraphs. An email message took shape on the screen.

He leaned over her shoulder to read it and was struck by

the sweet meadow hay scent of her. She smelled like…home. Her gasp pulled his attention sharply back to the computer screen.

…need you to position target on October first next to fountain, after supper but no later than ten-fifteen…

"What the heck is that about?" Alex murmured.

He didn't know, but he didn't like the sound of it. "Can you get the rest of that message?"

She shrugged. "Your father's hard drive hasn't been defragged in a while. We'll have to wait until the rest of that message gets read and sorted to see it."

He swore under his breath. His gut was vibrating in that ominous way it did when he'd just stumbled across something important. Hank was clearly supposed to set someone up for something. But what? A sales pitch? Assassination? And who was the target?

He thought aloud. "Are they talking about fountains in Washington?"

"If so, there are fountains on the Mall, and there's a big one at Dupont Circle, but those are outdoors. At 10:15 p.m. it will be dark and cold outside. I'm betting this note refers to an indoor fountain, then."

"What hotels or convention facilities in D.C. have fountains in their lobbies?" he asked.

She typed and, in a few moments, produced a list of venues in the Washington, D.C., area with fountains. He glanced through it and one leaped out at him. The Imperial Hotel. "Isn't there supposed to be a huge political fundraiser at the Imperial day after tomorrow?" he asked. "A big send-off before all the candidates head home for last-minute campaign sweeps?"

She frowned. "Let me check." She logged into his unit's

posting of significant VIP appearances around town for the week. "Yup. It's right here. The Imperial. October first. Everyone who's anyone will be there, including the president." She stared up at him, horrified. "This makes it sound like Hank was supposed to set up President Colton to be killed."

That was exactly what Hank had quietly told the authorities a while back, but Jim had been more than half convinced his old man had made the whole thing up to worm his way back into his family's good graces. Roscoe Harrington from McNaught had been inordinately interested in the Kelley family's personal connection to Joe Colton, though. Was the Raven's Head Society thinking about recruiting him to finish the job in his father's place?

Another encrypted document popped up on Alex's screen and Jim waited anxiously for the encryption to be broken. This one took several minutes. It was an outgoing message Hank had written to someone he called only R.

...can't guarantee anything. In spite of what you seem to think, I do not control J.C. Maybe I can deliver him, but odds are I can't. Suggest you formulate alternate plan."

Jim swore quietly. "J. C.—Joe Colton."

Alex's eyes went black with shock. "The Raven's Head Society *is* planning to kill the president."

"Looks that way," he replied grimly. Now the trick would be to learn enough about the assassination plot to stop it.

Over the next hour, a few more snippets of coded email came through and were duly decrypted. It became clear that Hank wanted no part of whatever assassination plot the Raven's Head Society was planning for the Imperial fundraiser. And it was just as clear his masters in the society had no intention of letting him off the hook.

Eventually, Alex asked, "Do you suppose his reluctance to help them is why Hank was shot?"

"Yes, I do. It also explains why Lana was kidnapped. They were pressuring Hank into cooperating with them."

"Why Hank?" Alex asked.

Jim's jaw rippled. "The Coltons and Kelleys go way back. If Hank asked Joe for a favor, Joe would do it, no questions asked. Not too many other people in this town can say that."

Alex nodded grimly. "Any idea how the Raven's Head Society plans to kill the president? Security will be ridiculous around the fundraiser. The hotel staff will be vetted out like crazy, and the guests will be all but strip-searched to get in."

"Particularly since the Secret Service has already been warned, and we're going to confirm that there's a specific threat against the boss at this affair."

They stared at each other, stumped. They both had the best training available anywhere in VIP protection. There just weren't that many ways to get to the President of the United States. His security detail was second to none.

Alex pulled up a schematic of the Imperial Hotel, and the reason for the choice of the fountain in the lobby immediately became obvious. The hotel was designed around a central atrium with the premium rooms opening onto hallways overlooking the atrium. It was a sniper's dream. Someone could take a shot at the president and melt back into a room before anyone had any idea where the shot had come from. Then it would be a simple matter for the shooter to dispose of the weapon, wash off the gunpowder residue and brazen out the security sweep to follow as if he were a regular guest at the hotel.

At midnight, Alex suggested Jim get a few hours' sleep while she babysat the remainder of the hard-drive recovery. After making her promise to wake him up if she found anything good, he stretched out on the sofa to catch a nap.

How much later a quiet exclamation dragged him from a deep sleep, he didn't know. But he came alert sharply and was on his feet all in one fast movement.

Alex was staring at her computer in dismay but was otherwise safe. "Don't scare me like that," he snapped. "I'm liable to shoot you next time."

She looked up at him, her gaze wide with dismay. "I know who's going to kill the president."

Chapter 8

Alex's stomach knotted at the way Jim surged up off the sofa, a warrior on full battle alert. She was such a sucker for soldiers. Or maybe just that particular soldier.

He moved swiftly to her side. "Talk," he ordered.

If he didn't stop being that macho and sexy, she was going to throw herself at him any minute and embarrass herself horribly. Sheesh. She must be more tired than she'd realized to be so distracted. She dragged her mind back to the crisis at hand.

"The Secret Service," she announced.

Jim frowned. "What about them?"

"That's how the Raven's Head Society is going to kill the president. From within his security detail."

"Are you crazy?" Jim blurted. "Those guys are scoped out so thoroughly they can't sneeze without someone knowing about it. Their loyalty is above reproach. They'll *die* to protect their man. No way has the Raven's Head Society suborned one of them."

"The Raven's Head Society has bought multiple congressmen. What makes you think they can't get their hooks into a single Secret Service agent?"

"My entire being rebels against that idea," he declared.

"Mine, too."

He said reluctantly, "Continue. Follow the logic."

She nodded and continued, "I was thinking. The only people who'll have weapons inside the Imperial Hotel will be Secret Service agents. Yes, it's far-fetched to think of one of them turning on the president, but it's pretty darned farfetched for this Raven's Head bunch to own senators and have the kind of financial clout the McNaught Group appears to. So, why not a Secret Service agent?"

She turned to her computer. "Once I allowed myself to consider that possibility, I started poking around the guys in the presidential security detail."

"How?" he asked incredulously.

She winced. "Let's just say I did a little extracurricular peeking in our unit's records to get their names and then went from there."

"You hacked into *our* security files?"

Under normal circumstances, she'd be thrown in jail for pulling a stunt like that. But these were anything but normal circumstances, and were becoming less so by the minute. She answered, "It's for a worthy cause, don't you think?"

He replied grimly, "Go on."

"So, I took a look at the financial records of all the men in the president's security detail. And I found something." She typed, bringing up the records of a bank account on her screen. "The guy's name is Walter Green. He's clean, but look at his mother's bank account. It's subtle. But check out these transactions."

She highlighted a series of payments to various doctors, hospitals and pharmacies. "For all the world, it appears that someone in the family is sick—cancer from the looks of it. And it also looks like Walter is footing most of the bill for the treatments. Or so it would seem."

He threw her a questioning look.

She continued, "I tracked down these payees, and none of them exist."

"How's that?"

"This hospital doesn't exist, and neither do these doctors or drug stores. These are fake transactions. The money's going somewhere else."

"Like where?" Jim demanded.

"I don't know. Offshore. Maybe Singapore. I haven't finished tracking down the money chain and I may not be able to quickly. The firewalls protecting these transactions are fantastic. When this is all over, I'm going to have to study them. Best security protocols I've ever seen—"

"Focus," he ordered her. "So this Walter Green guy is dirty?"

She shrugged. "There's definitely a very suspicious, and very well-hidden, money trail very close to him. And he's scheduled to work the Imperial fundraiser."

Jim swore under his breath and reached for his cell phone. She reached out and put her hand over his to stop him. His gaze jerked up to hers as their hands touched, and her pulse jumped in response.

"There's more," she said quietly.

He stilled, his big, warm hand resting beneath hers. It was all she could do to lift her fingers away from his. Her eyes strayed to his mouth. Memory of what it felt like to kiss those lips and be kissed back by them rolled through her.

"I took the liberty of letting myself into Mr. Green's computer," she said.

Jim's eyebrows shot up, but he made no comment. She shrugged in silent response. After the first felony of breaking into her unit's records, she figured another felony breaking into Walter Green's computer was no big deal.

"What did you find?" Jim prompted.

"He received instructions to finish the job no later than ten-fifteen and then take appropriate action." Jim started to reply but she waved him to silence. "Here's the kicker. Guess where the email originated?"

Jim propped a hip on the corner of the desk and crossed his arms. "Lay it on me."

"The White House."

She smiled reluctantly as Jim all but fell off the edge of the desk. "Are you kidding me?" he breathed.

"Would I kid about something like that?" she replied soberly.

"Where in the White House?" he demanded.

"I can't tell. Their security's a wee bit tough to penetrate."

Jim swore under his breath. "This Walter Green's orders to kill the president came from someone on the White House staff?"

"Looks that way. Which means you may not want to run right out and notify the Secret Service of the threat. For all we know, his orders are coming from inside the Service itself."

She waited out more quiet, but intense, swearing from Jim. Since she'd had a few more minutes to absorb the information and process it, she'd had a chance to consider how they should proceed next.

As he wound down into stunned silence, she suggested, "I think our best bet now is to have a little chat with Walter Green. Somebody's leaning on him—he may not be playing ball willingly. At least I'd like to think that no Secret Service agent would participate willingly in something like this. If that's the case, he may leap at the opportunity to tell someone what's up. Particularly if we've already pieced most of it together."

"Where's Green now?" Jim asked tersely.

"He's scheduled to come on duty at 8:00 a.m. That's five hours from now. So, my guess is he's at home asleep."

"You up for a little field trip?"

She was tired, but her adrenaline was pumping so hard there was no way she'd go to sleep if she lay down now. "Let's go."

She stood up at the same time Jim did and they came face-to-face abruptly. His hands came to rest on her shoulders. "You did good, Alex."

She lifted her gaze shyly to meet his. "Thanks."

He stared back down at her for an eternity. Long enough for her heart to trip and race. Long enough for her entire body to feel hot and flushed. Long enough for hunger to build deep in her belly and try to claw its way out of her. Jim's head bent. His mouth lowered toward hers. She didn't even stop to think about it. She lifted her mouth to meet his.

Their kiss was as natural as breathing. A blending of breath and lips and tongues, an exploration that rapidly expanded to hands speared into hair, her body dragged up against his, him pushed back down onto the edge of the desk, her riding his thigh and groaning at the sensation of his leg wedged against her throbbing core.

His arms tightened around her, and her breasts rubbed against his chest through their respective shirts. His mouth tore away from hers. She would have protested, but his lips closed upon her neck and burned a path of destruction down her throat to the hollow of her collarbone.

Meanwhile, his hot hands slid under the back of her shirt against her even hotter flesh, drawing her to his mouth and trapping her against him. Not that she had any desire to fight against the net of desire he'd so effortlessly cast around her.

Or maybe she'd cast it around herself. Who cared? She flung herself into the moment, hopelessly tangling herself in its invisible cords.

She hugged his head closer to her chest, reveling in the silky shortness of his dark hair. Restlessly, her hands roamed over his shoulders and neck, her fingers outlining his ears and finally tugging him back up to kiss her again. He surged to his feet, overwhelming her and surrounding her with his size and strength. Sometimes she forgot just how big and powerful a man he was. The idea of all that strength being directed at her, into her, made her legs go so liquid she had to cling to him to stay upright.

He swore against her mouth. "We've got no time for this."

She closed her eyes. Pressed her forehead against his chest. Frowned at the panting sound coming from somewhere nearby—oh, wait. That was her. "Do you have to be right all the time?" she groused against his shirt.

A finger under her chin tilted her face up to his. "Rain check?" he asked lightly.

She nodded. What else could she do? It was Jim.

He didn't release her hand as he led her from the suite, which was just as well. She was too befuddled from that steamy kiss he'd just laid on her to think, let alone walk with purpose. She followed him down into the parking garage and got into the BMW without comment. He started the engine and then glanced over at her wryly.

"You've got to quit looking like that, Alex, or I'm going to turn this car around and drag you back up to our suite to do something about all that smoking-hot sex your eyes are promising."

She blinked startled. "Uh, I'm sorry."

He laughed. "Never apologize for that, honey. Most men would kill to have a woman look at them like that. Hold that thought. Just save it for later, okay?"

She nodded, but it took most of the drive to Walter Green's tidy little house in the Virginia suburbs to compose herself even marginally. Smoking-hot sex with Jim Kelley? Every time the thought crossed her mind, she had to start the laborious process of calming herself all over.

The Beemer pulled to a stop in front of a neat, modest one-story ranch. "How do you want to play this?" she asked.

Jim grimaced. "The guy's armed and can handle a weapon. And if we're right about him, he's got to be nervous as hell. I'm thinking a polite knock at the front door would be our best bet not to die."

So much for sneaky commando tactics. Disgusted at yet again missing out on some real action, she got out of the car and followed Jim to the tiny porch. He rang the doorbell once. Waited a minute and rang it again. No lights went on in the house.

Nonetheless, Jim held up his military ID to the peephole and kept it there patiently. In a few seconds, the door cracked open an inch.

Jim didn't wait for anyone to speak. "Mr. Green, my partner and I work for the army. We have reason to believe you may be in some trouble. We're here to help, and we hope you can help us. We're tracking a group called the Raven's Head—"

The door was fully opened and a furious man stood there in boxer shorts and wielding a Colt .45 revolver in each hand. Alex reflexively raised her hands away from her sides as one of the big weapons was trained on her. Jim made the same gesture beside her.

"Shut up, you idiot," Green hissed. "Get in here."

Jim went first and Alex followed. Green waved them into a living room that opened off to the right of the small foyer. He gestured with the menacing weapons for them to sit on a sofa that all but swallowed Alex as she sank down onto it.

"What the hell do you know about the Raven's Head Society?" Walter growled.

Jim glanced over at her, clearly signaling her to take the lead. Surprised, she answered, "We have reason to believe they're blackmailing you into assassinating President Colton at the Imperial fundraiser in two days."

Walter staggered as if she'd struck him. But the guns never wavered. The guy was good. But then she'd expect no less of a man on the White House security detail.

"You have no idea what you're messing in," Walter hissed. "If you want to live, run, don't walk, away from this as fast as you can."

"We're here to help you—" Alex started.

The Secret Service man cut her off sharply with a wave of a revolver. He whispered urgently, "This thing is bigger than you can even begin to imagine."

"How much bigger?" Jim asked evenly.

Walter shook his head. Not going to spill the beans that easily. But then he surprised her by saying, "Raven's Head will always be one step ahead of you. They're smarter, richer, more connected than you can fathom. They have plans within plans. Nothing is ever as it seems with them. They'll chew you up and spit you out, little toy soldiers."

Although his voice never rose above a whisper, a note of hysteria rose within it. Clearly this guy was completely freaked out. It was hard to see much in the dim glow of the streetlights seeping in the front window, but the guy looked haggard. Stretched to the breaking point.

"Look," Alex said reasonably. "I know you don't want to go through with this plan of theirs. Talk to us. We can figure something out. We've got some pretty impressive resources of our own."

Walter laughed unpleasantly. The sound grated against her

ears and sent a shiver down her spine. "You're already dead. You're just too stupid to know it."

Jim spoke up. "How's that?"

Walter's gaze swung to Jim and they stared at each other for so long that Alex had to restrain an urge to fidget. It was as if the two men were having an entire conversation without ever uttering a word.

Finally Walter said, "You're here, aren't you? They've already seen you. Got you on their radar. And that means they're coming for you. They'll kill me for even letting you in to my house. Run. Right now. If you want to live."

Jim surprised her by standing up. As she rose to join him, Jim rattled off a phone number she recognized as that of his personal cell phone. "If you need anything, Walter, anything at all. Call me. Day or night. I'll help. You have my word."

The two men exchanged another long, grim look, two warriors recognizing their counterpart in one another. They exchanged brief nods, and then Jim glanced at her. "You heard the man. It's time to go."

They hustled to the front door, still wreathed in darkness. Jim paused in the act of reaching for the front door. "You leaving?" he asked their host.

"I'll do what I have to," was Walter's only reply.

Jim hesitated for a moment, then merely said quietly, "Let's go, Alex."

She strode down the sidewalk fast to keep up with him. They jumped in the BMW and Jim pulled away from the curb quickly, looking around nervously.

"What's going on?" she demanded.

"You heard the man. They're coming for us."

"You didn't seriously buy that line, did you? He was crazy." But something in her gut, something that feared Jim was right, forced her to add, "Who's coming for us?"

"The Raven's Head Society. And Walter Green is not crazy. He's dead and he knows it, but he's not crazy."

Alex stared at Jim incredulously. "Then why didn't we take him into custody? Our unit can protect him. We can trade his testimony for a trip over to the U.S. Marshall's office and a new identity. A new life. He'd be safe."

Jim shook his head. "You heard the man. Plans within plans. Nothing as it seems. The Raven's Head Society would find him. Kill him anyway. For all we know they've infiltrated the Witness Relocation Program, too."

She was missing something here. Something big. The key to what had just transpired. "What in the hell is going on, Jim?"

"We've stumbled into a rattlesnake nest. This thing's a lot bigger than I thought it was. Walter Green was right. The Raven's Head Society is coming for us. And if they catch us, they'll kill us."

Alex's stomach dropped as she stared at him.

He glanced over at her. "Looks like you got your wish, kid. You've landed smack dab in the middle of a combat op."

She'd always envisioned being part of a team with Hummers and automatic weapons and flak vests and night-vision goggles in some wilderness. Not zipping along I-495 in a BMW in jeans and a sweatshirt on her way back to one of the swankiest hotels in D.C.

Jim was speaking again. "We'll collect your gear and bug out of the Hays-Adam. It's time for us to go to ground. I'm not letting you get hurt."

She nodded, her head spinning.

As the first hint of dawn turned the sky gray outside, she stared around the walls of a tiny hotel room in Annapolis. She put down her bags of gear as Jim double-locked the door and wedged a chair underneath the knob for good measure.

"Now what?" she asked him.

"Sleep. We're going to need our rest over the next few days if I don't miss my guess."

She nodded, familiar with the first rule of field operations: eat and sleep whenever you can. You never know when you'll have another chance to do either. But then she glanced over at the narrow double bed and back at Jim's big body. It was going to be a tight fit. Her pulse fluttered.

She crawled under the covers while Jim pulled the black-out curtains shut and tucked in the edges. He lifted the bed covers and stretched out beside her. She was all but falling off the edge of her side of the bed, and still their shoulders bumped.

She tried rolling on her side with her back to him, but her elbows and knees hung off the mattress uncomfortably.

"Come here," he murmured.

"Excuse me?"

He held out an arm to her. "This is only going to work if we spoon."

Spoon? With him? He'd rolled on his side and was waiting for her expectantly. "Scoot back against me," he ordered.

In a second, she was snuggled up against Jim Kelley and his arm was draped over her waist, holding her close to his hot, hard body, his breath warm in her hair. And she was supposed to *sleep* like this?

"Mmm. Nice," he murmured.

She about leaped out of her skin.

"What are you so jumpy for? The bogeyman's not going to get you. At least, not while I'm here."

Her heart slammed against her ribs as his hand tightened, palm flat against her belly. After a moment, he commented, "I never knew what great shape you're in. Do you do anything besides kickbox and run?"

The words were out of her mouth before she could stop them. "I hear vigorous sex is a great aerobic workout."

Jim froze against her. Eventually, he muttered, "You shouldn't say things like that to a guy you're in bed with."

"Why not?"

"He'll think you're propositioning him."

"Do you?" God. Why did she keep blurting these things out? She had to get control of her big mouth and fast.

He rose up on an elbow behind her and she stared fixedly at the ugly gold wallpaper in front of her. His voice was low, charged. "*Are* you propositioning me?"

She'd waited her whole life for this moment. She was in bed with Jim Kelley and had a chance to tell him exactly what she'd spent most of her life dreaming of doing with him. And, of course, that was why her tongue suddenly and completely stuck to the top of her mouth.

He shifted his weight and pulled on her shoulder, rolling her partially onto her back so he could look down at her. "*Are* you?"

Chapter 9

Jim didn't know why he was holding his breath. It wasn't as if he'd never been in bed with a hot chick before. But never with a hot chick he'd known his whole life, whom he'd kill himself rather than hurt—*whoa*. Did he actually have *feelings* for her?

Alex opened her mouth. Closed it. Opened it again.

Oh, to hell with waiting for her answer. He leaned down and kissed her. Her lips softened and opened beneath his. Her arms snaked up to loop around his neck, and her upper body arched hungrily into his. That was all the answer he needed. He'd been lusting after her ever since he'd caught a glimpse of her in that sexy red ball gown, and she'd made no secret of her desire for him since…he thought back. Now that he thought about it, she'd pretty much always looked at him like that.

She was awkward and eager and rushed as he stripped off her clothes and his, and she was surprisingly shy about wanting the covers over them. How could a woman as beautiful as her not be highly experienced when it came to men? Not that he was complaining. He liked the idea that there hadn't been many men before him.

But when she kissed him with urgency approaching panic, he had a sudden realization. He propped himself up on an elbow to smile down at her. "Relax, Alex. I'm not going to change my mind about this."

She looked surprised and then embarrassed. He grinned and pushed her thick, dark hair back from her face. "Tell me what you like," he murmured.

"Uh, pizza. Coffee ice cream. White chocolate."

His smiled widened. She really was new at this. An urge to protect her, to make this really special for her surged in his gut, surprising him. He asked casually, "What's your favorite color?"

"Red."

No surprise there. Especially given the passion he now knew lurked just under her skin. "Where do you like to go on vacation?"

"Montana," she answered without hesitation.

He had to agree with her on that one. It was God's country up in the Rockies.

"Favorite sport?"

"Fishing."

He hadn't seen that one coming. "What kind of fishing?"

"Fly-fishing with my dad."

"Show me how sometime?"

"Next time we're back in Montana," she promised.

"Slow and easy or fast and hard?"

It took her a moment to figure out what he was asking. Her cheeks flamed. "Either. Both. I don't know."

He smiled gently. "Then why don't we find out together?"

Now that he had her talking he wasn't about to let her quit.

"Put your hands on me," he ordered. "Tell me what I feel like."

She plastered her palms to his chest. "Hard. Warm. I feel your heartbeat. It's faster than I expected."

That was probably because even this simple touch was turning him on a lot more than he'd expected it to. Her fingertips were wandering lower, but he managed not to roll over and ravish her on the spot. Barely. Her hands were small and soft as they explored his body. He had to grit his teeth when she grasped him rather boldly.

To his surprise, she muttered, "I don't think this is going to work."

And then he was laughing, gathering her in his arms, gently pushing her hand away before he exploded. Between chuckles, he said, "Trust me. It'll work just fine."

"Well, I'm sure everything *works,*" she huffed. "I just don't think it'll fit…well, you know where…" she trailed off. Her cheeks were scarlet in the faint light seeping around the curtains.

His laughter increased. "Yes, I know where, thank you very much."

"It's not funny—" she started.

He kissed away the rest of the sentence. He wasn't making fun of her. He just found her frankness refreshing. Completely and uniquely Alex.

"Shall we find out?" he murmured.

That struck her silent. But then he kissed his way across her shoulder and continued on to her belly, which was a bewitching combination of soft skin and firm muscle. He dragged his fingers up her calf, across the back of her knee, and up the long, slender path of her thigh to the center of the volcano she was rapidly becoming. Her breath caught on a little moan and he touched her again as he kissed his way to her breast and swirled his tongue around the tight peak he found there.

He waited until her entire body moved restlessly beneath him before he positioned himself and pressed slowly into her. Her eyes popped open in surprise and she stared up at him as their bodies slowly joined.

When he was seated to the hilt in her shockingly tight heat, he murmured, "What's the verdict? Is this going to work?"

She smacked his shoulder with the flat of her hand, but then he moved slightly and her attention was riveted once more. He withdrew slightly and then pushed forward. A groan escaped his throat.

And then she was talking once more, a steady stream of pleasurable sounds and exclamations as he demonstrated both slow and easy and fast and hard. As for his preference, he chose all of the above. She was miraculous, everything he'd ever looked for in a woman. But she was so much more, too. She was familiar, funny, someone he could be himself with. She was *family*. And all the protectiveness and affection that went with it surged in him. When she was all but incoherent, he paused and waited until her dazed eyes opened to stare up at him.

"Have we established that you like both slow and easy and hard and fast, then?" he asked.

This time the smack on his shoulder wasn't nearly as playful as before and quite a bit more demanding. The humor of the moment waned, leaving naked—and disconcerting—honesty pulsing between them. This was *Alex*. Someone to be cherished. The terror of their lovemaking shifted to a more tender note. He took a deep breath and slowed down to give attention to the details and maximize her pleasure. But in return, he found a sweetness, a satisfaction, in their joining that he'd never experienced before. Leave it to Alex to show him how little he'd really known about the woman until now.

As he fell back to the mattress, immensely grateful for the work out, Alex collapsed on top of him. Who'd have guessed she'd be quite so creative a lover when given half a chance?

He'd barely caught his breath before she pushed up onto her elbows and commented thoughtfully down at him, "Oh, and there's something else I'd like to try next time."

He grinned up at her. "Your wish is my command." He couldn't wait to see what she thought up next. He could spend a very long time enjoying her, in fact.

She rested drowsily on his chest and her breathing slowed toward the easy rhythms of sleep.

He couldn't remember the last time he'd been so comfortable with a woman. She fitted him. They had so much in common, so much history together. Strange how she'd been right in front of him all this time. "Why didn't we ever get together before now?" he asked reflectively.

"Because you couldn't be bothered to give me the time of day before you saw me all gussied up a few days ago," she murmured, half-asleep.

He froze beneath her, which had the effect of making her go alert, too.

"What?" she asked sharply.

"Do you really think I'm that shallow?" he demanded.

"Aren't you?"

"Then why did you make love with me?" Irritation laced his voice and he didn't bother to hide it.

"Like I'm ever going to have a chance to do this again with you?" she retorted. "The minute this op is over, you'll go running off after one of your usual blondes and we'll be old history."

"And you still jumped into the sack with me thinking that? Don't you have any more respect for yourself than that?"

She drew back, looking stung. "I—"

He never got to hear the end of what she was going to say

because that was when the door exploded inward, and in the cloud of smoke that followed, two masked men leaped forward.

Alex shocked him by rolling off the bed toward the attackers and letting her momentum carry her across the floor. He saw her tactic instantly and leaped forward low and hard himself. The gunmen would expect targets bed high. And the smoke worked both ways—it obscured the bad guys' vision, too. He dived below the first bullets that spat out of silenced guns. The bedding blew up behind him just as he barreled into the first man's knees.

The second assailant's weapon swung toward him, but Jim caught the fast-moving shape of Alex rolling into the guy, calf-high. Both assailants went down. In the tiny hotel room, it was an immediate tangle of limbs and bodies and weapons. He aimed his fists for anything clothed and prayed Alex could hold her own until he subdued the guy grappling with him. Frantic that she was too small and weak to defend herself, he went straight for his attacker's eyes until his man screamed once, a short, sharp sound Jim cut off with a hard blow to the guy's throat.

He dived for the man's dropped gun and whirled to take in Alex and her attacker. The man was behind her and had an arm around her throat, but Jim had turned just in time to see her reach back for the man's crotch. She got a handful of fabric and who knew what else and gave a violent twist. The man's arm jerked convulsively around her throat. Jim frantically searched for a clear shot, but the guy released Alex, shoving her so hard she slammed into the side of the bed.

Jim didn't hesitate. He double-tapped the trigger, aiming straight for the man's heart. As the assailant on the floor rolled to take a shot, Jim spun and neutralized him for good, too. Thank goodness they'd had sound suppressors on their weapons. The last thing he and Alex needed was for the police to show up and demand explanations that would take the next several days to unravel.

He lurched forward to draw Alex into his arms, to make sure she was all right, to keep her from going hysterical and bringing everyone in the hotel down on them. But mostly, he needed to reassure himself that she was okay. That he could go on living.

Instead, she surprised him by shoving away to run her hands over his arms and down his ribs. "Are you hit?" she bit out.

"I'm fine," he answered, shocked at her composure. "You?"

"Fine. Throat's gonna be sore for a day or two. We need to get out of here."

"Are you all right?" he asked. "Truly? Two men just tried to kill us."

She spoke tersely. "I'm not some wilting lily who wrings her hand at a mouse or a spider. I am a trained soldier and military technician, if you recall. And we have work to do. If it'll make you feel better, I'll go all girly and weepy on you later. I promise. Now help me search the bodies."

Predictably, neither man carried ID of any kind. They both had disposable cell phones on them, but no phone numbers were programmed into either device. Still, Jim pocketed both. Maybe they'd get lucky and someone would call them looking for a report on the hit. He threw the bedspread over both bodies on the floor.

He and Alex dressed quickly and slipped into the hallway. The Do Not Disturb sign on the door ought to buy them twenty-four hours or so.

As much as he loved his car, they had to ditch it. He drove them out to Dulles Airport and parked it in a crowded, long-term parking lot holding plenty of other BMWs, and they rented a less-conspicuous replacement car at one of the counters in the main terminal.

He drove into the cell-phone parking lot on the airport property and made a phone call to Austin Kittredge. "Kelley here. I need a secure line."

"You're on one, Jim. What's up?"

"Alex and I just ran into a little trouble. Two armed men burst into our hotel room and tried to kill us."

"Say status."

"We're fine. They're dead."

A long silence greeted that. Then merely, "Roger. Say intentions."

"If they're trying to kill us, we're on to something. Alex and I found a Secret Service agent with some financial irregularities. We think he's being blackmailed into trying to assassinate President Colton at the Imperial fundraiser tomorrow night."

"Walter Green?" his boss asked grimly.

"How do you know about him?" Jim blurted.

"He's dead. Appears to have hanged himself sometime last night."

Jim swore violently. Walter had warned them to run. Had maybe saved their lives by doing so. "We saw him at about 3:00 a.m. He was alive and not suicidal. Scared of—no, resigned to—dying but not looking to kill himself. Ten to one it's murder and not suicide. I can't imagine he went down without a fight. Have you got eyes on the crime scene?"

"Working on it," his boss replied. "We'll up the threat status with the Secret Service—"

"No!" Jim said sharply. "Whoever was leaning on Green did it from a White House computer. The Secret Service may be compromised."

That provoked a very long silence on the other end of the line. Finally, "What are your intentions, Jim?"

"Alex and I are making progress. Let us run with this. Meanwhile, you bring in a team of our security personnel to supplement the presidential security detail at tomorrow's fundraiser. At any cost, don't let Joe Colton get anywhere near the fountain in the lobby of the Imperial Hotel tomorrow night."

"Done. And you two be careful. Report in when you can." The line went dead.

Jim felt as if a weight had been lifted from his chest now that his superiors were in the loop and the president would be protected. And then Alex asked, "Are you sure you can trust whoever you were just talking to?"

"Of course—" he started. But she didn't need to say it for him to know what she was thinking. If the Raven's Head Society could get inside the White House itself to launch a hit on the president, was any branch of the government beyond their reach? Surely not Austin Kittredge. They'd known each other for years. Worked on countless life-and-death missions together. Hell, saved each other's lives a time or two.

"I trust you," he finally said.

Alex gulped. She trusted him, too. But the realization hung heavy in the air between them that from here on out, they were on their own. They didn't know who to trust and who not to trust. The Raven's Head Society conceivably had its claws into anyone and everyone they might come into contact with.

She asked, "Can we go back to the unit and pick up a few more pieces of equipment to help me decode the encryptions my computer couldn't crack off your dad's hard drive?"

"I don't think we'd better," Jim answered heavily.

They truly were alone, then. She nodded. "If we can find a decent electronics store, I should be able to find all I need to cobble together a workable decryption protocol."

●

"I don't know how on earth you'll do that, but I believe you," Jim replied dryly.

She smiled at him wearily. "Thank goodness you're finally letting me do my job."

"How 'bout we find someplace to hole up for a while and catch a nap?"

Her cheeks heated up. They'd tried the whole sleeping thing earlier but hadn't gotten much in the way of rest. Not that she was complaining. She would remember making love with Jim Kelley for the rest of her life. It had been everything that she'd ever dreamed and more. She didn't care what he'd said about her not having any self-respect. She would never regret sleeping with him.

But a little voice tickled the back of her mind in warning. Okay, maybe she might regret it. But she was still glad she'd done it. She'd happily face whatever consequences came of it. The little voice warned her ominously to be careful what she wished for.

Jim pointed their rental car toward northern Virginia and surprised her by paying cash for a motel room less than a mile from CIA headquarters. He grinned as she stepped past him into the room. "No one would dare try to bug a place like this. Too many visiting spooks as customers. They'd catch it in a minute."

She nodded, suddenly exhausted by the sight of a big, inviting bed.

He tucked her in with a chaste kiss on the forehead. She appreciated his consideration for her state of fatigue. She was asleep before his hand lifted away from the blankets.

Jim stared down at Alex sleeping peacefully. She looked about twelve in her sleep. He flashed back to summers at the ranch. He and his brothers and Arty running around like maniacs with her tagging along behind, always trying to keep up with the older kids. She and Lana had been close until the accident, and Alex had mostly hung out with the boys after that.

He'd thought she wanted the comfort of being with her brother's best friend. Shared loss and all. But, in retrospect, he wondered. After that awful summer, it was almost as if she became one of the pack of boys tearing around the ranch. She'd tried so hard to take up the empty space Arty's death had left in them all. She might as well have been wishing for the moon, though. There was no replacing a young life snuffed out just as it began to unfold.

He turned away, stripping his shirt off over his head as exhaustion pulled at him. The last day had been a hell of a roller coaster, starting with that call from Alex announcing that she was being followed and possibly set up for kidnapping, and ending with assassins bursting into their hotel room.

He sat down on the edge of the bed and kicked off his shoes. Funny how, after everything, his mind didn't stray to who wanted to kill them. It wandered back to the sounds Alex made in the throes of pleasure, the amazed smile on her face, the way her eyes sparkled and snapped like black diamonds when she laughed. Arty would be so proud of how she'd turned out.

And then it hit him. He'd slept with his best friend's little sister. If Arty were alive, he might be proud of Alex, but he'd kick Jim's ass for messing with his sister. He dropped his head into his hands. What the hell had he done? That was Alex. The kid he'd grown up with. Who'd followed him and Arty around like an eager puppy. Who'd worshipped her brother and transferred that worship to him when Arty had died.

And he'd just taken advantage of her in the worst possible way. She'd admitted freely to knowing he would dump her as soon as this op was over. And he hadn't said a damned thing to contradict her. Sure, a pair of assassins had cut the discussion short, but it hadn't been in his mind to contradict anything she'd said about him. His only reaction had been to be indignant that she'd called a spade a spade to his face.

He glanced over at her. One slender shoulder was visible above the edge of the blanket, her honeyed skin smooth and sleek. God, he was a cad. She deserved better than this. Much better. Bleakly, he swung his feet into the bed and drew the covers up over himself. How was he ever going to make it right with her? He'd crossed one of those lines with her from which there was no going back. His last thought before he crashed into unconsciousness was that he'd really screwed up big this time.

Chapter 10

Alex woke to the sound of the motel room door opening. She rolled and was on her feet in a defensive crouch all in one movement.

Jim glanced up at her from the doorway, a grocery bag in his arm. "Stand down," he blurted, startled.

She straightened, her heart pounding. "Don't scare me like that," she declared. "You should've let me know you were going out. If I'd woken up and found you gone, I'd have freaked out."

He set the groceries down on the fake-wood-grain Formica table in the corner. "Looks like you freaked out plenty well without me waking you up first."

"Whatever." She scowled and rubbed her face with her hands. "What'd you get for breakfast?"

"Make that supper. We slept all day."

She glanced at the window and was surprised to see only fading light creeping around the curtains. "Yeah, well, surviving an assassination attempt has that effect on me."

"Speaking of which, I picked up ammunition for the extra pistols we lifted off the killers. We're well-armed now."

"And who are we planning to kill?" she asked as she reached for bread, deli meat, sliced cheese and mustard.

He considered her. "I was thinking more in terms of self-defense, but you pose an interesting question. How do we proceed from here?"

She shrugged. "First order of business is to decrypt the remaining files on your father's hard drive and see what we get."

They gulped down a bite to eat and then Jim drove her to an electronics superstore. She picked up the supplies she needed and they returned to the motel room. It was a fairly simple matter to set up a decryption program to work on the remaining files from Hank's hard drive.

Jim seemed withdrawn and thoughtful and sat propped up against a pile of pillows on the bed while she watched the computer do its thing. Gradually, something strange dawned on her.

"Jim," she asked, "why did the Raven's Head people go to all the trouble of erasing Hank's hard drive and then leave it behind for us to find?"

He looked up at her sharply.

"Doesn't that seem just a little too convenient? That guy, Walter Green, was clear that the Raven's Head Society is smart. *Plans within plans,* he said. Why did such smart folks leave the drive behind? It's Computer Security 101 to take the entire hard drive out if you don't want someone to see the information stored on a computer."

Jim was on his feet beside her in an instant. "You mean this is a wild goose chase?"

She stared up at him. "I think we're supposed to get side-tracked chasing down whatever we find on this drive."

He nodded grimly. "Okay, then. What's the false lead they're trying to make us follow?"

She looked down at the papers that had already printed out. "Most of these have to do with the campaign. But the interesting ones hint at some sort of plot to assassinate someone important, presumably the president."

"Plans within plans," Joe muttered. "If killing President Colton isn't their real goal, then what is?"

She tapped a tooth with a fingernail. "If you wanted serious power, what would you do?"

"I'd invest until I was so rich I could buy anything or anyone I wanted to."

"From the looks of the McNaught Group's financial records, the Raven's Head Society has already done that. Once you've got that kind of power, what would you do with it?"

Jim frowned. "I'd take control of key industries. Manipulate stock markets, maybe push around the economies of various countries."

"To what end?" She was intensely interested in watching Jim's mind work like this. He'd come a long way from the wild kid bombing around the ranch in a pickup truck.

"I'd want to advance the interests of my own country, or maybe of my own political point of view."

"So the ultimate expression of power would be politics for you?"

He shrugged. "Not politics per se, but controlling how people—entire populations of people—think. And I suppose politics and religion are the two most obvious ways to do that."

She nodded. "The Raven's Head Society doesn't seem overly involved with religion, so we have to assume they've chosen politics as their method for controlling public opinion."

He continued her line of reasoning. "The single most powerful politician in the world is the President of the United States."

"Then why would they try to kill the president?"

Alex's gaze snapped up to Jim's. Obviously, the exact same thought that had just occurred to her had also occurred to him. She said slowly, "They want to kill the president because they don't control him. They want to put someone in office whom they can control."

Jim finished the thought for her. "The vice president."

"I did find reference to Metzger in a few McNaught documents. Looks like they already have their hooks into him."

He nodded reluctantly. "It's the logical conclusion."

She finished the thought. "Then they're trying to kill President Colton to get him out of the way."

"Except you and I know they won't succeed in killing him tomorrow night. The Secret Service will see to that. So the big question is what will their plan B entail?"

"I have no idea, except that it will be smart and subtle."

He sighed, agreeing. "We've got one day to figure it out."

Thing was, she didn't have the faintest idea of how to begin. For lack of any better ideas maybe, her mind strayed to the other implications of that single day looming before them. It was the only day they had left to work together. And then her fantasy mission with the man she loved would be over. Done. And somehow she would have to find a way to go on with the rest of her life.

"What about their money?" Joe said abruptly, startling her out of her dark thoughts.

"What about it?"

"Is there some way we can hit the Raven's Head Society in its wallet?"

"Not legally."

"I'm not so concerned with legality. I just want to stop these bastards."

"Hacking into banks is a great deal more difficult than they make it out to be in the movies. It can take months to bypass a single firewall. And by the time you get past it, they've put up a new and improved one behind it." She added dryly, "Turns out people take protecting their money very seriously."

He snorted. After a moment, he said, "What if we didn't actually hit their money, but just made them think we did?"

"What purpose would that serve?" she asked curiously.

"Psychological warfare."

"Are you sure you want to provoke these folks that way? They've already tried to kill us once."

He shrugged. "It's just something to think about."

He moved over to the window to stare out at the trees behind the motel. She turned over his idea in her head, pondering how she'd fake a massive financial upheaval. Eventually, she said, "I'd hit a major stock market."

He turned. "Come again?"

"I'd start a rumor that a major financial market was on the verge of collapse. You wouldn't have to do anything to the actual trading computers. You'd only have to hack your way into the reports of stock prices. People would panic if they thought stock prices were plunging."

He gestured for her to continue.

"The McNaught Group, which we believe to be the front for the Raven's Head Society, is heavily invested in a specific portfolio of stocks and financial instruments. I would target those particular stocks with a hack. I would falsely report all of those stocks to be plunging in value all of a sudden. You could panic the living daylights out of everyone in the McNaught Group."

He paced, thinking. "I doubt Austin Kittredge would give us permission to mess with a major stock market. But it would be a great way to find out exactly who's involved with the Raven's Head Society. Just watch everyone you suspect send out your false data, and see who panics."

She shrugged. "I'm just saying. It could be done."

"I'll keep that in mind. The first order of business has to be protecting the president from the Ravens' plan B."

Idly, she fooled around with typing up software to invade the reporting systems of a dozen major international stock markets. It wasn't that hard, really. The worst of it would be getting past the 256-bit encryptions. In a perfect world, she'd turn the job over to the FBI. They no doubt had access to the right passwords, not to mention the federal judges and stock market officials who would have to approve such a stunt.

After a long, tense silence, Jim turned to her, frustrated. "I've got nothing, dammit! We've got to figure out what their backup plan is!"

"Maybe we should go back to the unit and tell the gang what's up. They're a smart bunch. They'll have plenty of ideas. And protecting people like the president and figuring out ways someone might try to harm a VIP like him is what all of your men are trained to do."

"Yeah, but it was my sister these bastards kidnapped."

She replied quietly, "That doesn't give you any special right to hoard this case all to yourself."

He glared at her and snapped, "How do we know my unit's not compromised? We can't tell anyone what we know."

"That's a cop-out. The Raven's Head Society doesn't own everyone. Odds are they've got one, maybe two guys, in your entire command structure. The vast majority of your colleagues are entirely trustworthy."

He scowled fiercely at her. "Yes, but we don't know which one or two guys it is. And until we do, I'm not talking to anyone."

She subsided, disturbed. Jim was too personally involved with this case. Was he losing perspective on it? "I think," she said slowly, "this thing may be too big for just the two of us. Plots to assassinate the president? Taking down a bunch of stock markets? We're in over our heads here. It's time to bring in the big guns."

"And how will we know who to trust?" he demanded.

That was the question of the hour, now, wasn't it?

Jim paced the tiny motel room restlessly. It was frustrating as hell knowing so much about his foe, and yet being so in the dark as to the Raven's Head Society's next move. What were the bastards up to? With the death of Walter Green, surely their assassination attempt was compromised—unless they had a backup shooter, which would certainly be their style. Still, these people had to be supremely cautious. They hadn't risen to the kind of wealth and power they had in complete secrecy by being brazen about anything.

The assassination attempt at the Imperial Hotel fundraiser had undoubtedly already been scrubbed. Which meant plan B was probably already in play. Like it or not, it was time for drastic action. He was going to *have* to talk to someone, no matter how loudly his gut was yelling at him not to do it. Maybe they could ask some questions, get some help, without giving away everything they'd learned and suspected. It was the best they could do. Time was too short for them to sit around staring at their toes until they came up with a brilliant theory of what the Ravens would try next.

"Alex, if I got you help from the White House I.T. staff, could you figure out who in the White House sent those messages to Hank ordering him to get Joe Colton to the fountain at ten-fifteen?"

She glanced up from what she was typing, startled. "Absolutely. But how do you plan to get their help?"

He reached for his cell phone. "I'm going to ask."

"Who do you trust?" she challenged.

"I don't have to trust whoever we ask for help. I just have to ask him an innocent enough question that it won't trigger any alarms or make the Ravens think we're on to them."

"And you're confident you can pull that off? The Raven's Head Society doesn't strike me as that easy to trick."

He grinned. "Won't know whether we can do it until we try."

She just shook her head at him.

He dialed information, and an electronic voice recited the White House switchboard number at him. He dialed it, and in moments a pleasant woman was asking how she could direct his call.

Several of his colleagues from his unit had made the jump to civilian jobs in the White House Security Office over the years. It was an option he might even consider when it was time for him to retire. The man he'd randomly picked of the those he knew was at the office today, and the operator put Jim through to the guy's desk.

"White House Security."

"Hey, it's Jim Kelley."

"Jim! How the heck are ya, man?"

"I'm great. Hey, I need your help. I need to speak with someone in the White House I.T. office. Any chance you can patch the call through and let them know I'm not some crackpot cold-calling off the street?"

His former soldier laughed. "I dunno about the crackpot bit. I always wondered about you...."

Jim laughed back. "Go to hell."

"Just a sec. I'm going to put you on hold while I ring the computer guys."

Jim waited impatiently. One minute stretched into two and then into three. Finally a voice came on the line. "White House I.T."

Jim explained briefly that he needed a little help from their office to track down the source of an outgoing email whose address tag had gotten cut off in transmission. He got passed off to someone else and repeated himself. He was passed to a third someone and put on speaker phone to explain himself. He was starting to worry that his story of the dropped address tag was wearing thin. He launched into his story yet again but was startled when a voice abruptly cut onto the line.

"Jim Kelley? Hank's boy?"

"That's right. Who am I speaking to?"

"Joe Colton. I was passing by the desk and heard your name. How's Hank? Any change?"

Holy crap. The president in person? Hastily, Jim answered, "No, sir. They're still waiting for the swelling in his brain to come down before they try to wake him up."

"He's in my prayers. Tell your mother that for me, will you?"

"Of course, Mr. President."

"What are you calling here for, anyway? Something we can do for you?"

"Yes, actually. I was sorting through my father's correspondence and he received an email from a White House computer. I'm trying to track down who sent it so I can follow up on some business for him. I was calling to ask if the White House I.T. staff could help me."

"Consider it done, Jim. I'll let Martin, here, take care of the details. If there's anything else I can do for your family, give me a buzz."

He rattled off a phone number quickly enough that Jim barely caught it. As Jim repeated it to himself a few times to remember it, Colton added, "Good talking to you."

"You too, sir."

Across the room, Alex's jaw was hanging open. Jim muttered to her, "Sometimes you get a lucky break."

"That's a word for it," she retorted.

A man came on the line and Jim explained briefly that he was going to pass the phone off to his computer expert. He shoved the phone at Alex. In seconds, she was animatedly speaking computerese with the geek on the other end. She rattled off a series of letters and numbers, listened for a moment, and then…and then the strangest thing happened. She paled.

He'd have thought a person with her golden complexion couldn't go that sheet-white, but apparently he was wrong. She disconnected the line and passed him his phone in stunned silence.

"What's up?" he asked quickly.

"You'll never guess who sent those messages to Hank."

He frowned. "Who?"

"President Colton. The messages came from his personal computer in the White House residence. Martin told me no one but the president has the password to that system."

Jim felt his own face drain of blood. "Joe Colton sent the messages ordering my father to set up his own assassination? That's crazy. It must be a mistake."

"No mistake. The I.T. guy double-checked it for me. The president of the United States is trying to have himself killed."

Chapter 11

Alex felt as though someone had just punched her in the gut. What in the heck was going on around them? It was as if she was a piece of foam being tossed on an angry ocean called the Raven's Head Society. She didn't care what Jim said. The two of them were in way over their heads and needed help. Jim's need to be a hero, to bring to justice his sisters' kidnappers, to protect his family, was overriding his better judgment. She was tempted to contact Austin Kittredge on her own and question whether Jim should be working on this mission at all.

Of course, if Jim ever found that out, he'd kill her. Flat out. He'd made it his personal mission to nail his sister's kidnappers and nothing and no one was going to stand in the way of that. Not even her. No matter if they'd had epic sex together. His obsession would still win out.

Depressed, she did a few mild calisthenics in the corner to get her blood flowing. It had definitely not been the smartest thing she'd ever done to jump in the sack with Jim Kelley. At least not in his current frame of mind. She wasn't some naive teenager. She'd known he was distracted. Was she the bad guy here? Had she taken advantage of him to get what she'd wanted? She feared that was the case. No doubt about it, no repeat performances were in the cards for them if she knew what was good for either one of them.

She happened to glance up and caught Jim watching her stretch, his gaze blazing with...something. She dared not give it a name, for unfettered lust was the only thing it could be. He looked away quickly, and she did the same. Right. No more smoking-hot sex for them, no sir. But her body disagreed violently as aching heat rolled through her and left her knees, no kidding, weak.

She swore under her breath.

The computer worked through the night, but none of the files it decrypted shed any more light on President Colton's bizarre scheme to kill himself. In the wee hours of the morning, exhausted and her nerves so jangled she felt ill, Alex crawled into bed. Jim turned off the lights and followed suit.

Uncomfortable didn't begin to describe how awkward she felt lying in the same bed with him. His body crept across the space between them, tantalizing her, but she'd be twice damned before she would give in to the need rippling through her.

They plastered themselves to their respective edges of the mattress, backs turned to one another, and pretended to sleep, but she suspected he wasn't getting any more rest than she was. When her body wasn't humming with frustration, her mind was shouting in even worse frustration at not knowing what the Ravens were up to. She hated the idea of being outsmarted by anyone, particularly when peoples' lives rode on it.

When the sun finally peeked around their curtains, Jim

was the first to give up the pretense and jumped up to pace the room. She held out a few seconds longer for appearances' sake, but then rose and headed for the shower.

They choked down fresh fruit and hunks of cheese for breakfast and slugged juice straight from the carton.

Jim broke the tense silence by announcing, "We have to go shopping again."

She looked up sharply. "Why? We've still got food."

"We need formal clothes. Unfortunately, I'm not James Bond. I don't haul a tux around with me in my emergency overnight bag."

She laughed. "And why do you need this tuxedo?"

"We have a fundraiser to go to this evening at the Imperial Hotel."

She jolted. They were going to the scene of the crime in person? Her pulse leaped.

They drove to a nondescript bridal shop where Jim rented a tuxedo that fit him better than any rented clothing had a right to. She shopped hastily for another gown, half-panicked in Carla's absence. She settled on a black number too slinky to look like a mother-of-the-bride dress.

They spent the afternoon figuratively banging their heads against the wall. What were the Ravens up to? What was the president up to? Or was Colton being set up? Or blackmailed? By whom? How? Why? No matter which way they attacked the problem, they just kept coming up with more and more questions.

As the sun set, Alex wrestled her way through curling irons and makeup all by herself. It was perhaps more daunting than the prospect of coming face to face with would-be assassins tonight. The good news was she wasn't aiming for Hollywood bombshell tonight. Security agents blended in with their surroundings. The eye passed over them without really registering them.

She gave herself one last critical look in the mirror. Her hair fell in soft waves and her makeup was subtle. Still, her eyes looked big and dark, and even the hint of lip gloss made her smile pop. She had to admit, she didn't look half-bad.

She slipped into the pair of blessedly low-heeled black satin pumps from the bridal store. Of course, they were still probably a death trap waiting to happen.

Jim's voice floated in from the bedroom, startling her. "Time to go."

Jim jolted as Alex stepped out of the bathroom. The physical impact of her beauty crashed into him. She'd played down her looks tonight, but it didn't stop his heart from slamming against his ribs when he looked at her. It was as if once the blinders had come off all he could see was her beauty. She could probably have stepped out in sloppy sweats and a ponytail without a lick of makeup and he'd have been dazzled by her.

Who was he kidding? He couldn't just walk away from her as though nothing had ever happened between them. Never again would he look at her without wanting to put his hands on her, wanting to draw her into his arms and kiss her until she made those sweet sounds at the back of her throat, wanting to make her keen her pleasure against his neck.

"You look spectacular," he said soberly.

"Too spectacular?" she asked anxiously. "I tried to tone down what Carla did before. I don't want to attract too much attention tonight. Should I go take off some of the makeup?"

He laughed shortly. "Honey, there's not a thing you could do to prevent men from noticing you. They're going to be drooling all over you."

"Maybe I should stay outside. I can work surveillance and support while you go to the party."

"Not a chance. You're coming with me and that's that."

He was shocked to realize he wanted to show her off again. To be the guy with the ravishing brunette on his arm and to be the envy of every man at the party.

She moved over to him and reached up to straighten his bow tie. Of their own volition, his hands touched her upper arms, drifting downward wistfully. God, he missed her. Which was weird, given that she was standing right here. He realized he missed being naked beside her. Feeling her smooth skin against his.

Tough, he told himself grimly. Get over the woman. She's not for you.

A belligerent whisper in his skull demanded to know why not, but he ignored it. The stubborn little mental bastard just wouldn't let it go.

"You grow more lovely every time I look at you," he murmured.

"So you're going blind, then?" she asked lightly. He thought she sounded a little out of breath, too.

"Not hardly." He bent down to brush his lips lightly across her cheek. Just a casual thing between friends. Except all of a sudden her mouth was there, his mouth crushed against hers, and she was kissing him back as though she was drowning and he was her lifeline. While the rational part of his brain swore frantically and ordered him urgently to stop this madness, the little whisper beneath was smug. *That's more like it.*

He was in serious trouble. It was only with the greatest of effort he managed to tear his mouth away from hers. "I don't want to ruin your hair and makeup," he rasped.

"And we can't be late," she added in desperation.

Not good. She sounded as lost in lust as he was. He took a stumbling step back. His hands fell away from her. They stared at one another for a long, charged moment, breathing hard.

"Uh, right, then," he mumbled.

"Right. Time to go," she mumbled back.

But the atmosphere between them was so heavy with tension he could cut it with a table knife. Why was he walking away from a woman who wanted him that badly? What kind of damn fool did something like that? What did it matter if she was his best friend's sister? Arty was dead.

Quick guilt speared through him. Dead because Jim hadn't insisted on his buddy sitting back down and putting his seat belt on. He'd told Arty to quit horsing around hanging his head out the window, but he could've pushed the point harder. Maybe if he had, Arty wouldn't have been ejected from the truck when it rolled down the embankment. Maybe he'd have had the truck's heavy frame to protect him from the trees he'd slammed into as he'd flown down the mountain. Maybe he wouldn't have died in a broken heap that would haunt Jim for the rest of his life.

Well, hell. Alex had stepped away from him and looked crestfallen. He was the mother of all asses. He'd hurt her feelings by mentally drifting and seeming to reject her, and she hadn't done a darned thing to deserve it.

"C'mon, beautiful," he said jauntily. "I want to show off my girl to everyone in Washington."

Her dark gaze snapped to him, hope gleaming for just a moment in her wide eyes before she masked the emotion. Oh, yeah. He was definitely an ass of the first water. She so deserved better than this. Better than *him*.

The drive to the Imperial Hotel was silent, each of them lost in their own thoughts. Knowing her, she was thinking through every scenario that might present itself tonight and contingency-planning her way through them all. He ought to be doing the same. But instead, he couldn't shake the image of her gazing up at him, vulnerable and hurt. Hurt he'd put there.

Austin Kittredge had arranged to get the two of them on the guest list of the fundraiser, and Jim suspected Kittredge hadn't forked up thirty grand each to do it this time. They left their weapons in the car and had no trouble passing through the full-body X-ray machines and into the party, which was already going strong when they arrived.

A crowd milled in the lobby around the large, multitiered fountain. Jim glanced around casually, taking in the numerous outstanding sight points for a sniper in the hallways ringing the upper reaches of the atrium. What a nightmare.

He led Alex into the Grand Ballroom, which already held several thousand guests with more arriving every minute. One advantage of the crush was their relative anonymity. He and Alex moved through the crowd undisturbed. As he'd expected, though, most of the men gave Alex a thorough up and down. She was a knockout and that was all there was to it.

He spotted several of his troops scattered through the crowd and more of them strategically placed in the corners of the room. At least with his Secret Service on high alert he was less worried about the president's life. Odds were low that the Raven's Head Society had managed to suborn more than one agent in that group. Frankly, it was a miracle they'd gotten to Walter Green.

"Do you see them?" Alex murmured under the din of the crowd.

"My men?" he replied.

"No. The McNaught people."

He looked sharply in the direction she indicated. Roscoe Harrington, the man he'd been eating lunch with the day Alex had called to tell him she was being followed, was standing with several other men he recognized from the McNaught roster. Ernie Bradshaw, CEO of the largest privately held insurance company in the country, also had his head together with the McNaught types. Bradshaw would be quite a feather in the Raven's Head Society's cap. The guy was worth billions.

The men didn't seem to have spotted him and Alex, so he steered her away from the group. Cruising the party became a little trickier as they spotted two more clusters of McNaught people, presumably Raven's Head members.

Dinner was a drawn-out affair. The food was good but nothing to write home about, the speeches delivered during the meal about the same. The hands on his watch seemed to be moving at half speed as they crept toward ten o'clock. But finally, the meal ended and the guests stood to let the waiters clear the room. By unspoken mutual consent, he and Alex drifted out toward the hotel lobby and the fountain.

No surprise, several McNaught types were strategically placed around the expansive lobby. Here to see the show, were they? Macabre bastards. It was hard to keep an eye on the balconies overhead without seeming to do so. He and Alex took turns gazing around the cavernous space, but it was the best they could do.

"See anything?" he murmured.

"No. You?"

"Nothing—" He was about to add that this was a good thing when a disturbance at the far end of the lobby drew his horrified attention. He swore violently. "I told them not to let him out here—"

He broke off, grabbing Alex's hand and dragging her toward the President of the United States as he emerged into the Imperial lobby and headed straight for the fountain.

"What's he doing?" Alex gasped, spying the president. "I thought your guys weren't supposed to let him out here!"

"So did I," he growled.

He reached the fountain and started left around it to block the president from reaching it and ideally to tell the guy's security detail to get him the hell out of here right now. But the distinctive spit of a silenced, low-velocity round being fired from a high-powered weapon rang out, and Jim leaped on Alex, smashing her to the marble floor.

Two more wheezy, spitting noises erupted. Most of the patrons either didn't hear the shots or didn't know what the sounds were, for they stared in confusion at the few people who'd inexplicably dived for the floor around them.

"The president!" Alex grunted from beneath him.

Jim's brain shifted into some sort of weird slow motion. Why hadn't he dived for Colton? Why had his instinct been to cover Alex and protect her from harm? His mind registered that now was not the time to consider such things, but it filed the questions for later. His brain moved on to the problem of saving the president. He had to get to Colton. Make sure the president was alive. Unharmed. Help give the Secret Service detail the cover they needed to get the president out of here to safety.

"C'mon," he shouted at Alex as people finally began to realize something bad was happening and screaming and shouting erupted. They had only seconds before pandemonium ruled, and then protecting the president would go from nightmarish to outright impossible.

Alex seemed to understand the urgency of the moment as well. "Through the fountain!" she shouted in his ear.

He nodded and pushed to his feet, reaching down to drag her up beside him. They jumped over the low lip of the water feature and splashed forward, in a high-kneed dash. Jim rounded the center pedestal and his blood ran cold at the sight that greeted him.

The president was down, cradled in the arms of several of his Secret Service agents while two more lay on top of him. Four agents had their weapons drawn and were searching upward frantically, seeking a target to bring down. To no avail apparently, for none of their weapons had rung out with deafening fire.

Jim threw his hands up in the air and shouted to the nearest Secret Service man, "I'm Captain Jim Kelley! Army Supplemental Security Unit. Can the principal be moved?"

The Secret Service man spared him a glance and nodded tersely. "Backup's en route. There's no goddamned cover in here!"

Now was not the moment for I-told-you-so's. He'd warned his men to keep Colton out of here. That message surely had been passed on to the president's personal detail. Dammit, he'd *told* them.

In seconds, no less than twenty big, armed, fast-moving men burst into the lobby. The main Secret Service contingent. They bulldozed a path to the scrum covering the president, and Jim and Alex were shoved back as the team surrounded their man and whisked him out of the lobby toward the ballroom, and likely a rear exit.

Police burst in through the front door of the hotel, and the general panic deepened as the crowd finally caught on that something very bad had just happened.

Jim plastered his mouth against Alex's ear. "Let's get out of here. Otherwise, we'll spend all night being questioned by the police."

She nodded and they ran for the front door along with any number of other panicked patrons. A wave of them burst past the police and out onto the street. They'd made it. They ran for a couple of blocks until the cacophony of sirens and noise in front of the Imperial Hotel had receded behind them.

"Now what?" Alex murmured.

Jim's gaze narrowed. "Now we take a chance."

"How so?" she asked curiously.

Throwing her a dark look, he pulled out his cell phone and dialed Roscoe Harrington's cell phone. It was noisy in the background when the guy picked up. He must still be inside the hotel.

"Harrington, it's Jim Kelley. I did as you people asked my father to do and got the target out to the fountain on time. Now, I want in to the Ravens. I'd say I've earned it, wouldn't you?"

As he'd expected, stunned silence met his declaration. Finally, Harrington responded, "I don't know what you're talking about."

Jim laughed shortly, without humor. "Don't bullshit me. You know exactly what I'm talking about. I want in. My father's toast, but I want to take his place."

"I'll be in touch," was all Harrington said.

Jim disconnected the call. Alex was staring at him in disbelief when he glanced over at her. "What?" he muttered.

"Do you have a *death* wish?" she demanded.

"No. But I'm damned well catching the bastards who kidnapped my sister and just may have killed the president."

Alex pulled out her cell phone and started typing rapidly into it. She waited a moment and then announced, "The first reports are that someone took shots at the president, but they're not reporting any injury to him."

"Joe Colton could be dead and his people wouldn't tell the press a thing."

She sighed. They both knew he was right. It was standard protocol when a VIP went down to keep all information about it from the media.

They walked in silence for a few more minutes before Alex muttered, "I knew if I wore heels tonight I'd end up having to run in the darned things."

"Sorry. At least you're not falling down as much as you used to."

His cell phone vibrated in his pocket and he whipped it

out to look at it. "Harrington," he murmured as he accepted the call. Alex went tense and still beside him.

"I hope you're calling to tell me what I want to hear," he said into the phone.

"We need to talk, Jim."

"I bet we do," he replied dryly. "I know this isn't how things are normally done, but these aren't normal times. My father's dying in a hospital and who the hell knows if Joe Colton's alive or not. Extraordinary times call for extraordinary measures, don't you think?"

Harrington made a noncommittal sound and then surprised Jim by rattling off an address. The man finished with, "Be there in an hour."

"You've got it," Jim replied eagerly.

He pocketed his phone and looked over at Alex. "We're in."

Chapter 12

In to what? Alex asked herself that question yet again as she looked doubtfully at the apparently deserted rows of warehouses looming around them. "This looks like a setup," she murmured to Jim. "Are you sure they're not planning to kill us?"

Jim shrugged. "We'll know when we get there."

She really was starting to worry about how he seemed to be wearing blinders where the Raven's Head Society was concerned. He seemed so hell-bent on nabbing them that his judgment was becoming questionable. "How about we call in a little backup? Maybe a few guys from the unit to come over and protect our line of retreat?"

Jim threw her a withering look. "We can handle a meeting with a few dried-up old men who pull other peoples' strings for fun."

"But what if that's not who's waiting for us?"

"Then we'll handle it. You wanted a real field op, right? Welcome to the big leagues, Mendez."

She reeled back from him. She was Mendez again? So much for their brief affair. Apparently, it was over. Agony speared into her gut. She told herself grimly she'd better get used to the pain because this was a taste of her future to come. She might have had Jim for a brief moment in time, but he was lost to her now. She wanted badly to double over, clutch her middle and moan out her pain and loss. But now was not the time. And besides, it was her own darned fault.

Jim had paused in front of a door and was looking left and right. "This is it," he murmured. He drew his sidearm and she did the same. "I'll break right. You break left," he breathed.

"Roger. I'm left," she repeated.

Jim tested the doorknob; the door was unlocked. He eased it open and slipped inside low and fast. She followed suit, spinning to place her back to the wall as she crouched, scanning the left half of the space before her. It was very dark, but she made out the shapes of high shelves lining wide rows. Totally clichéd warehouse layout. Pallets were stacked high overhead on the metal storage racks. A forklift was parked not far away.

"Clear," she whispered.

"Clear," Jim replied under his breath.

She stood up and realized her legs felt weak and wobbly. She recognized the telltale signs of an adrenaline rush. Exultation shot through her. This was what she'd been waiting for. Real field experience.

Jim moved off to his right and she sidled along the wall after him, keeping her gaze and her weapon moving at all times. For a place where there was supposed to be a meeting, this warehouse was darned dark and spooky.

"Why aren't the lights on?" she whispered to Jim.

He shrugged and kept moving. She frowned. Was she

just inexperienced, or was Jim not operating at full speed? Sure, he was the experienced operator and ought to know if anything seemed shady or not. But still, her internal alarm system jangled nervously.

He moved around the edge of the space, pausing to peer down each new row as they approached it. Their contacts either hadn't arrived yet or were acting very strangely.

They rounded yet another corner and Alex caught a flash of movement out of the corner of her eye. Jim froze as if he'd seen the shadowed figure, too. He hand-signaled her to stay close. He took off running down the long tunnel of the row and she raced after him, cursing her shoes yet again. It was a pain in the butt running on her toes so her heels didn't click on the concrete floor.

Jim paused at the end of the row and crouched low, peering slowly around the corner. He pulled back and signaled her. One man. Armed. Moving away. And then Jim signaled for her to stay here and take cover. She stared in disbelief. Was he *kidding*? They had a tactical advantage two-on-one. But if Jim took her out of the action, the odds dropped to fifty-fifty, him against the shooter.

She shook her head sharply in the negative and signaled back that she would peel off to the left and try to flank the shooter.

Jim's hand slashed angrily through the air and he repeated the signal for her to stay put.

She shook her head back at him. It was career suicide to disobey orders in the army, and doubly career suicide to do it in combat. But Jim was dead wrong. He was trying to protect her, and he had to get over it. She was a soldier, same as he was. And she could handle herself under fire. At least she was pretty sure she could. She might be a rookie, but she was smart and motivated. That had to count for something, right?

She slid back down the row a few feet. Jim signaled her angrily to stand down. She looked him in the eye as best she could in the near total darkness, trying to convey her apologies and her determination to do her job whether he wanted her to or not. Resignation blossomed in his gaze.

She nodded her acknowledgement and he scowled briefly. There'd definitely be hell to pay later for this. But in the meantime, he signaled her to circle left and flank from that direction. *Yes.* Eagerly she repeated the command back at him and then moved off into the dark.

But when she was alone, creeping through the rows of crates, her heart about pounded out of her chest. The guys in the unit said a person got used to the danger after a while and learned to control the fight-or-flight terror reaction. But at this moment, she found that very hard to believe. One foot in front of another, she crept forward. Accidentally she let a heel down too hard and it clicked on the concrete. She froze, cursing female footwear in general.

She crouched for a full minute, but nobody came charging around the corner, guns blazing, to take her out. In disgust, she slipped off the shoes and proceeded in her stocking feet. Although it was eminently quieter, her nylons were horrendously slippery against the smooth floor. Sheesh. A girl couldn't win for losing. She stopped long enough to shimmy out of her panty hose and prayed the few seconds' delay wouldn't prove costly to the mission.

Finally barefoot and silent, she moved on. One, two, three aisles she crossed. Estimating that the shooter was around four aisles away from Jim the last time she'd spotted him, she approached the fourth row cautiously. Mimicking Jim, she crouched low and tipped her head just far enough around the corner for one eye to clear the shelves. The aisle was deserted.

She darted across the aisle and repeated the maneuver as

she approached the fifth aisle. Except this time the space was not deserted. A shadow stood at the far end of the tunnel-like space, a compact semi-automatic assault weapon clutched in front of him.

No doubt about it. The Raven's Head Society had sent them here to die. Jim should be in position to do whatever he was going to do by now. She waited in an agony of suspense for something to change in the tense stand-off. This encounter was Jim's to control. She might have insisted on playing ball, but he was calling the shots.

As the seconds stretched out, the tension in the warehouse grew exponentially. Something had to happen and soon. She leaned forward to check on her man and her stomach dropped like a stone. The shooter was gone.

She turned the corner and raced toward the guy's previous position. Where had he gone? Had she lost him? Was Jim vulnerable, believing she had him covered when she didn't? Crud, crud, crud. She approached the spot where the shooter had been standing moments before and looked around frantically.

Something big and dark dropped down from overhead and crashed into her, knocking her violently to the ground. Her head cracked into the concrete and she saw stars as something cold and hard pressed into her right temple.

It didn't take any field experience at all to know that was the muzzle of a pistol shoved against the side of her head.

"Get up. Slowly," the shooter ordered in a whisper.

She complied, her mind racing frantically. Where was Jim? How could she stay out of her partner's line of fire? And how was she going to keep this guy from shooting her dead in the next few seconds?

"Are you the guy from the Raven's Head Society that Harrington sent to meet us?" she asked in a normal speaking voice.

"Shut up," the shooter hissed.

She cast about desperately for something to distract this guy from the index finger of his right hand. If he squeezed the digit, she was history. She said companionably, "I bet you're the guy who shot the president, aren't you? Busy night you're having. I hope the Ravens are paying you great. You're really, really good to have made it out of the Imperial before the police or the Secret Service caught up with you. How'd you do it?"

"Took out a window and rappelled down the side of the building," the man answered, glancing around nervously.

"That's awesome," she blurted. "I'd love to work with you sometime. Pick up a few pointers."

That got the guy's attention. "Excuse me?"

"This is a job interview, right?"

"What the hell are you talking about, lady?"

"Let me guess. The Ravens sent you here with orders to kill us. Right? Well, my partner and I were sent here with orders to stop you from killing us. If we succeed, then we get promotions within the Raven's Head Society."

"The who?"

She nodded knowingly. "Of course. You're a contract worker. They wouldn't have identified themselves to you by name. Who's your contact with them?"

"Harrington."

She nodded. "Busy little camper, Roscoe. If you don't mind my asking, what did he pay you to kill Joe Colton?"

The shooter's gun jerked slightly against her skull. "I didn't kill Colton. I had orders to take torso shots only. No-where that wasn't protected by a bulletproof vest." The guy's voice rose in dismay. "I didn't kill him, did I? The deal was Harrington wouldn't pay my family if I killed the president."

"Naw. He's fine. You did great," she answered. Alex's head spun. This man was supposed to merely have staged killing the president? Was Colton indeed trying to *fake* his assassination? What on earth for?

Aloud, she asked, "And Walter Green? Did you kill the Secret Service agent, too? Nice bit of work. The police still think he killed himself."

The man in front of her grinned, his teeth gleaming white in the darkness. "Thanks. Although he didn't put up much of a fight. Seemed ready to die. Almost glad to get it over with. Tired of running, I guess."

Alex's stomach turned. How could this man speak so casually of ending another man's life? Green had been a decent guy. Trying to do the right thing.

"Drop the weapon!" Jim's voice rang out in the darkness.

"Yeah, whatever," the shooter replied, standing up and leaning his automatic weapon against the crate beside him. "You win. You get your jobs with your fancy Society. Tell Harrington I said you two aren't half-bad."

Alex spied Jim advancing down the main aisle, his pistol still cradled cautiously in both hands before him, aimed squarely at the shooter. She prudently stayed down on the floor and well out of any possible line of fire.

"Who are you?" Jim demanded.

The guy snorted. "Does it matter? I assume you're here to make sure I finish the job. You bastards are cold, you know that? Sending the replacements to finish off the previous schmuck. One word of advice: watch out for that last job with Harrington. It's a bitch."

Alex frowned. What was this guy talking about?

The guy smiled and from close range like this, Alex thought she detected a little madness in the expression. Maybe it was just the weird angle of looking at him from the floor.

The man reached for a pistol in his waistband, yanked it

out fast and, as Jim's weapon came up to bear on him, the man slammed the muzzle into his mouth and pulled the trigger.

The explosion was deafening. Alex scrambled frantically, scooting away on her bottom from the crumpled body of the dead man before her.

"Holy Christ!" Jim exclaimed, sprinting forward. "You okay, Alex?"

"I'm not hurt. What the heck just happened?"

Jim knelt beside the man briefly. "He's dead. Killed himself."

"That was his last job? To blow his own brains out?" Alex asked blankly.

"Apparently. He thought we were here to make sure he did it." Jim glanced over at her where she huddled, shaking violently. "We've got to get out of here."

"Ya think?" she managed to mumble.

Jim held a hand down to her and she took it numbly. He dragged her to her feet. "Don't step in the blood."

"The police will know from the spatter pattern that someone else was here," she retorted.

"No help for it. Just don't leave them enough forensic evidence to make finding us easy." He added grimly, "The good news is the Raven's Head Society probably expected that poor guy to kill us before knocking himself off. Which means as long as we lie low we've got a window to operate while the Ravens believe we're dead."

Yippee. She was dead now. She scooped up her discarded shoes and pantyhose and nodded numbly, following Jim down the aisle toward the exit. She felt as if she was swimming through molasses and her mind wasn't moving any faster. Must be shock. She and Jim slipped outside into the silent alley. It was bizarre how nothing out here seemed to have changed in the least. But a man had just killed himself a few yards away. How could the night be so unaffected? She shivered and followed Jim toward their rental car.

She roused from her zombie state, though, when the sound of a quiet engine and crunching gravel split the silence behind them. Jim swore and took off running. She followed suit. So much for the Raven's Head Society believing they were dead. Harrington and company *had* sent someone to verify that their man had killed himself after all. And the backups had just spotted her and Jim.

She dived into the passenger's seat of the car as Jim revved the engine and peeled out, making no attempt at secrecy. Sure enough, a big, dark SUV careened out onto the street behind them. Jim swore under his breath and concentrated on guiding the vehicle at high speed down city streets not designed for this sort of driving.

"Call Kittredge," he bit out. "Tell him we found the president's shooter."

She pulled out her cell phone and dialed the number Jim gave her.

"Mendez?" Kittredge seemed startled to get a call from her.

"How's the president?" she asked urgently.

"Bruised ribs where the vest took a couple of bullets, but he'll be fine."

She relayed the good news to Jim. The shooter had done his job, then, and only hit Joe Colton where he was wearing body armor.

Kittredge was speaking, "...how come you're calling? Everything okay?"

"Jim's in the middle of a high-speed car chase at the moment. He can't talk. We found the guy who shot President Colton. In a warehouse in southeast D.C. He's dead. I think the weapon he used to shoot Colton is with him. You can have your forensics guys verify it."

"What the hell happened?" Kittredge blurted.

"Jim set up a meeting with the Raven's Head Society. When we got there, an assassin was waiting for us. We talked with him and he admitted to killing Walter Green and shooting Colton. Then he stuck a gun in his mouth and blew his brains out."

"Oh my God," Kittredge said thickly. "I'll send the FBI over." A short pause. "Who's chasing you?"

"The Raven's Head Society, presumably. Roscoe Harrington's men."

"Harrington's directly involved in wet ops for them?"

"Looks that way."

"He didn't strike me as the type to get his hands dirty."

Alex frowned. "Me, neither. He must be getting orders from higher up. And if his bosses are making him do stuff this out of character for him, they must be getting nervous."

"What support do you two need?"

"I dunno. Lemme ask Jim." She held the receiver away from her mouth and relayed Kittredge's question.

Jim frowned but didn't take his eyes off the road. They skidded around a corner with a squeal of rubber like a Formula One car. The vehicle fishtailed slightly before he got it straightened out and accelerated once more. Then Jim snapped, "I don't trust anyone at this point. Tell Kittredege we'll handle it."

Alex stared. "We've got killers literally on our tail and you're going to turn down help? Are you crazy?"

He glanced over at her, his eyes blazing. "I'm in charge, and I say no backup. I'll handle it."

Reluctantly, she put the phone back up to her ear. "You catch that?" she asked Kittredge.

"Is he okay?" Jim's boss asked anxiously.

"No."

"What's going on, Mendez?"

"Later," she replied.

"You'll call me later when you can talk out of Jim's hearing, then?" Austin asked her tersely.

"You've got it, sir."

"I'm going to brief in a few men I trust, anyway. Keep an eye on Jim for me until I get them up to speed and they join you. I'd hate to have anything happen to him."

Yeah. So would she. She hung up glumly. What the heck was she supposed to do now? How was she going to keep Jim safe from himself? Would he even let her if she tried?

Chapter 13

Another wild turn slammed her against the car door and she was forced to concentrate on not getting thrown across the car for the next few minutes.

They pulled out onto a stretch of highway and Jim stomped on the accelerator. The vehicle leaped forward eagerly, quickly outdistancing the heavier and slower SUV behind them. Alex had driven from D.C. to Annapolis on several occasions, but never, ever, had she made the trip in a matter of minutes. She was thankful that the hour was late enough for the usual Friday-night traffic to have thinned out significantly. Still, occasional drivers honked their horns at Jim as he wound in and out of the sparse traffic at nearly a hundred miles per hour.

They hit Annapolis proper and were forced to slow down radically on the narrow and winding streets of the old town. He guided the car into the crowded parking lot of a bar that was still open. Finally she was able to take a minute to grab a handful of fast-food-restaurant napkins from the glove compartment and mop herself more or less clean of blood from her proximity to the earlier shooting.

"C'mon," Jim ordered.

She jumped out of the car and raced after him as he sprinted for the banks of the Chesapeake Bay. They followed the waterfront for several blocks, and then Jim dodged onto a pier without warning. She followed him toward an eight-foot-tall hurricane fence and an imposing gate blocking access to the luxury yachts and sailboats beyond.

"The top of that fence looks electrified," she muttered. "Surely you're not planning on climbing it."

"Oh, ye of little faith," Jim retorted. "I know the security code for the marina. We're going in through the gate."

Sure enough, he keyed in a number sequence and the wrought-iron gate swung open in a few seconds. They slipped into the darkened marina and locked the gate behind them.

"Evening," a male voice said from behind them.

Alex whirled, startled.

Jim answered easily, "Hey, Sam. This is my friend Alex. Hal and Steph gave us the keys to their boat for the week. We'll be hanging around the pier for a couple of days."

The guard mumbled something about them enjoying themselves and moved on.

"This way," Jim murmured. He led her quickly down a long pier to a slip holding a fancy-looking sailboat. At the moment all the sails were packed away and the mast towered, tall and naked, overhead.

She jumped across to the deck of the vessel and followed Jim to a narrow door leading below deck. He did, indeed, produce a key and let himself inside. She followed him curiously.

The ceilings were low and the space compact, but every amenity looked accounted for. Bathroom, kitchen, table, bed.

She slipped into the banquette seat next to the table with a sigh of relief. Finally. Some breathing space. She opened various closets to find them neatly stacked with life vests, canned foods and, praise the lord, clothes.

"Would your friend mind if I borrowed some pants and a sweatshirt?" she asked over her shoulder.

Jim answered from over by television, where he was flipping through news channels. "Take whatever you need. Steph would be mad if you didn't."

She slipped into the tiny bedroom to change out of the black dress, which was ruined. She tried on a pair of their absent hostess's tennis shoes and was delighted to discover they weren't an awful fit. Alex vowed she wasn't going to get caught in high heels again in the middle of an op for as long as she lived. She stepped out in time to see Jim move to a porthole and peer out cautiously past the curtains.

"You think they can find us here?" she asked, dismayed.

"I think we'd be foolish to underestimate the Ravens."

He was right—and maybe she could use that to talk some sense into him. "Jim, these people are really powerful. The two of us aren't going to be able to bring down the whole organization by ourselves. We've got to get help. We'll figure out a way to know who to trust."

He shook his head sharply in denial. "We're close, Alex. Don't wimp out on me, now. You wanted a field op and now you're getting it. This is what it's like sometimes—kill or be killed."

Except she was desperate not to see him killed. He wasn't just some soldier she worked with. This was the boy she'd spent every summer with for her entire life. Her brother's best friend. Her first crush. Hell, her only crush. And briefly, he'd even been her lover. She woke up every morning thinking about him and went to sleep at night thinking about him. When she was ninety-two, she suspected she'd still be dreaming of what could've been with him. No way could she sit by and watch him die. She just didn't have it in her.

"I get all that macho kill-or-be-killed stuff. But I still think the Ravens are too much for us. You and I both know that overwhelming quantity wins on the battlefield over quality every day of the week and twice on Sunday. The Ravens have resources we can't even begin to match, let alone counter. Bring in the FBI. The police. The Secret Service. Let's take these guys out, but let's do it in a way guaranteed to bag the whole organization. We're going to have to match their power with power of our own."

"You don't have any idea what you're talking about," Jim snapped.

She bristled. "I hate to burst your bubble, Tarzan, but I've got a college degree in strategic planning, and I *do* know what I'm talking about."

He spared a glance away from the window at her. "Book-learning and real-world experience are entirely different animals."

"Agreed. But certain fundamental principles have held true ever since Sun Tzu first wrote about the art of war two thousand years ago."

He snorted. "You're not seriously going to quote Sun Tzu at me, are you? There are guys out there trying to hunt us down and *kill* us with weapons and technologies Sun Tzu couldn't possibly fathom."

"At least you finally grasp the gravity of our situation," she snapped back.

He answered implacably, "Get some sleep. I'll take first watch."

He obviously considered the conversation over. She cursed under her breath. He was wrong about going solo on this mission. She was dead sure of it, deep down in her gut. Huffing, she stomped to the bedroom and crawled into the wedge-shaped bed.

Tomorrow she'd find a way to get through to him. She *had* to.

The almost subliminal rocking of the boat beneath her lulled her to sleep shockingly fast in spite of her ire at her partner.

Jim sat on the teak deck, leaning back against the pilot-house in the darkest shadow the sailboat had to offer. No way could he sleep. His nerves had been a short-circuited wreck ever since he'd spied that guy in the warehouse pointing an automatic weapon at Alex.

Although, truth be told, he'd been freaked out since the moment that first shot had spat out in the Imperial Hotel and his reflex had been to jump on Alex, not to leap for Joe Colton. What was *wrong* with him?

Alex didn't even want a relationship with him. She'd made it perfectly clear it had been a one-night stand and she expected no more than that from him. He ought to be relieved that she understood how these things worked, right? Most bachelors would give their right arm to find a woman who gave them the hottest sex they'd ever had and wanted nothing in return.

He'd scratched the itch, and now he could move on, no muss, no fuss, no strings attached. Alex really was the perfect woman.

Then why was his gut knotted up so tight he could barely swallow? And why did the prospect of her casually moving on to some other guy make his face go hot and his jaw tighten until it ached?

He never went in for this possessive he-man crap. He was more mature than that. And that was why he only dated grown-up women who understood the score. He showed them a good time, spent a lot of money on them and in return they got a casual hookup. But they knew not to expect more.

What about Alex, though? She seemed a little freaked out by his wealth, if anything. He'd had no chance at all to lavish her with gifts and expensive dates, although she didn't seem to care that he'd omitted either. As for expecting no emotional entanglement, though, she'd gotten that one spot-on. Thing was, had he?

Could he just move on from her? He'd known her forever. She was part of the bedrock of his life in the same way the Kelley ranch was or his family was. They'd always been there and always would be. He might have ignored her over the years, first because he was too young to know what to do about her, and later out of respect for Arty, but the truth was he'd always known Alex was sweet on him. That, too, was part of the fabric of his life, a thread woven through all his memories of growing up.

He'd spent the entire school year every year antsy to get back to Montana. He told himself it was because he loved the mountains. But in retrospect, he'd lied to himself. There was more to it than that. Alex had always been there, scrawny and puppy eyed, tagging along behind him worshipfully, her loyalty to him unswerving over the years. It had been one of a very few constants in his life.

While his dad was busy dragging him and his siblings back and forth between California and Washington, marching them out every campaign season to pretend perfect family harmony for the voters, he'd always known Alex was in Montana, patiently waiting for his return.

And she'd gone and grown up into an intelligent, interesting woman who was actually comfortable in his world. He'd been stunned when she'd shown up in his unit as a support technician. And if he was being brutally honest with himself, he'd been thrilled to see her. It was as if a little piece of home had landed on his doorstep.

And then she'd had to go and shock him senseless with her unexpected metamorphosis from caterpillar to butterfly. Although, truth be told, she'd been a butterfly for a long time now; he'd just been too stubborn to acknowledge it. Even tonight, with her makeup sweated off and her hair a mess, she'd still been so beautiful he could hardly take his eyes off her. There was something about her. A quality of inner calm, confidence, certainty of who she was and how she felt, that appealed to him intensely.

What in the hell was he supposed to do about her? He *hated* having her out here with him in danger. He wanted to send her somewhere far away from here. Somewhere safe where he wouldn't have to worry about her. Where he could dream of coming home to her waiting arms and being wrapped up in comfort and happiness. Except he couldn't imagine not knowing whether she was safe, wondering if the Ravens had gotten to her when he wasn't around to protect her.

Instead of being tucked safely into her own bed tonight, she was out here getting guns pointed at her and running for her life. He was failing her miserably.

He swore under his breath. But what choice did he have? He'd vowed to Hank, as his father lay near death in the hospital, that he would catch Lana's kidnappers. Like it or not, he needed Alex's help if he was going to keep his promise. And he didn't break his promises, dammit.

Three o'clock came and went and Jim's eyelids finally began to grow heavy. He slipped inside the cabin and moved through the dark to the bedroom. He paused beside the bed to gaze down at Alex. She was curled on her side with her fists tucked under her chin. She looked about the same age she'd been when her brother died.

He flashed back for a moment to the funeral. How his heart had completely broken at the sight of the tears running silently down her cheeks. She'd never made a sound, though. She'd just stood there ramrod-straight beside her sobbing father, holding in her agony for her pop's sake. So strong she'd been, even then. Always doing what was necessary for the people she loved and ignoring the cost to herself. In retrospect, that had been the moment his feelings changed about her.

At seventeen and wallowing in the guilt of having not done something more to save her brother, he'd put his new feelings for her down to protective impulses. He'd felt a need to step into Arty's place for her, to be the big brother she'd lost. But now, looking back, he wondered. Had his feelings been more than simple brotherly love, even then?

Alex shifted in her sleep, rolling onto her back. He reached down and touched her shoulder gently. She jolted upright, sitting up and gazing around wildly.

"Bad dream?" he murmured.

She shoved her tangled hair off her forehead, swearing quietly. "Is it my turn for the watch?" she mumbled.

"Sorry. I'm getting a little ragged. I only need a couple of hours of rest, though. Then you can go back to bed."

She rolled off the side of the bed and loss stabbed his gut. Avoiding him, was she? He sighed and moved to the foot of the bed to intercept her.

"I'm sorry for everything, Alex."

She frowned up at him. "*Everything* as in what?"

Hell if he knew. He shrugged. "I'm just sorry. If you get tired, wake me up."

She turned and left, leaving him alone to his melancholy thoughts. God, he'd really screwed things up between them. And worse, he had no clue how to fix it. She'd pulled away from him emotionally, and he hadn't the faintest idea how to bridge the chasm.

It was light out when Alex shook him urgently from a dead sleep. "Get up, Jim. You've got to see this."

Half-awake and disoriented by the adrenaline surging through him, he stumbled into the main room. A tiny television mounted high on the wall was broadcasting a morning news show.

The anchor announced, "Information has surfaced in the wake of last night's alleged assassination attempt of President Joseph Colton that indicates Colton himself may have been behind the attack. Sources say orders were passed to a rogue Secret Service agent who killed himself a few days ago to arrange for a hit man to shoot at the president…"

Jim's jaw sagged. "How? Who?" he spluttered.

Alex looked as appalled as he felt. "We were the only people who knew what was in those emails to your father from the White House. Well, us and Austin Kittredge."

Jim swore violently and snatched his cell phone out of his pocket. He jabbed the numbers for Kittredge's home.

His boss came one the line, sounding sleepy.

"Tell me you didn't leak the information about the White House emails to the press," Jim demanded angrily.

"What?" Austin sounded as though he was waking up fast.

"Turn on the news." Jim waited impatiently while his boss did so. Through the phone line, Jim heard another account of the allegations against the president, this report adding slyly that Colton's numbers had been slipping in the polls and hinting that the president might have arranged a fake hit upon himself to drum up sympathy among voters.

Austin said forcefully, "I swear, Jim. I didn't tell anyone the specifics of what you and Alex found."

He heard the genuine horror in Austin's voice. The guy had to be telling the truth. "Who then?" Jim asked.

Austin answered grimly, "The only other person who would know about those posts is the person who sent them. Surely Joe Colton didn't leak this stuff to the media. It would be career suicide."

Jim growled, "You're assuming Colton wrote the letters. We don't know that." In fact, the more he thought about it, the more certain he was that Colton was being set up. "'Plans within plans,'" he blurted.

"I beg your pardon?" Austin asked.

"It's something Walter Green said about the Raven's Head Society. He said they have plans within plans. If they can't kill the president, maybe they can frame him for the assassination attempt. They can kill the guy's credibility and make him a lame-duck president two years early."

Austin said heavily, "Switch to the *Comstock Show*."

Jim did as his boss suggested and watched in dismay as the news analyst called for impeachment hearings against Joe Colton if the allegations of faking an assassination attempt turned out to be true.

Austin said quietly, "Why settle for a lame duck if they can get the guy thrown out of office?"

"Victor Metzger," Alex said abruptly.

Jim glanced over at her questioningly.

"If the Ravens can get President Colton kicked out, their man will become president."

Austin was grimly silent at the other end of the phone. He must've heard Alex's comment. Finally his boss said, "Let me help you, Jim. We've got to bring these guys down. Now. Before they get their hooks into the Oval Office itself. What can I do?"

"Let me think about how to proceed," Jim replied. "I'll call you back."

The problem was, the Ravens knew how to deal with big, powerful organizations. They got inside and rotted them from within. His instinct was to stay tiny. Mouselike. Slip under the Raven's Head/McNaught radar. The fewer the people involved with this investigation, the more likely they were to be able to slide past the Ravens' notice. But the temptation was large to call in the cavalry and throw everything Uncle Sam had at these people.

He paced the tiny confines of the living area, wrestling with the best course of action, but was brought up short when Alex murmured from the doorway, "Is it normal for two men in business suits to walk into a marina?"

Jim leaped to the hatch and peered out where she pointed. He didn't recognize either man, but he definitely recognized the type. Hired muscle. The marina's day watchman pointed in the direction of the pier he and Alex were tied up to.

"Time to go," Jim bit out. "Do you scuba dive?"

"No," Alex wailed under her breath.

"You're about to get a crash course." Jim threw open the locker holding Hal and Stephanie's scuba gear and threw a wetsuit, fins, a mask, a weight belt and an oxygen tank at Alex. "Put these on. Breathe in and out through your mouth only." He checked the gauges on both air tanks. "We've got ninety minutes of air. We'll plan to stay under for sixty minutes. Check your watch. If we get separated, don't forget to check the time often. Don't go deep. You don't know anything about decompressing properly."

She staggered up the steps behind him, her fins flopping crazily. The two suits were just hopping onto the boat two slips down and disappearing from sight. She stumbled into Jim and he muttered as he emerged on deck, "Stay low and turn around. It's a lot easier to walk backward in fins."

They probably had only a few seconds before the men emerged again.

"Slide into the water as quietly as you can," he directed. She nodded and he gave her gear one lightning-fast check before he put the regulator into her mouth and turned on her tank.

And then they were easing into the murky water of the Chesapeake. The cold shock of it stole his breath away. Visibility was terrible—only a few feet. He grabbed Alex's hand and gave it a squeeze. She gave him a squeeze back and he gave a mental sigh of relief. Plucky woman.

He pointed into the narrow channel between piers and she nodded. Grateful for their weight belts, he swam for the bottom with Alex in tow. Then, kicking strongly through ten or twelve feet of water if his ears weren't lying, he crossed the open water, hoping against hope that their pursuers weren't looking for streams of bubbles in the water. No bullets zinged randomly into the water around them, so maybe they'd made it. He wasn't about to surface and find out, however.

He revised his estimate of how long they could safely stay in the water. It was colder than he'd expected. With the wetsuits, he figured they had ten, maybe fifteen minutes before hypothermia set in. With that in mind, he ducked under the next row of sailboats and crossed the next channel of the marina before he turned out toward the bay proper.

Sunlight glowed dimly through the green gloom, and an oily sheen marred the surface overhead. As they cleared the marina, a mild rip current tugged against them, trying to suck them away from shore. Not exactly pristine conditions for scuba diving.

He fought along, never letting go of Alex's hand and squeezing it from time to time to check on her. Each time she returned the squeeze. He was so proud of her.

They followed the shore until he was starting to cramp up and Alex was shivering so violently he could feel it through her hand. And then he spied his goal—another marina. There weren't too many places where people could emerge from the bay in wetsuits without drawing tons of attention. He was hoping to find a boat to break into to take cover in. They needed to dry off and warm up before they did anything else.

He crawled onto a pier and dragged Alex up beside him. They lay beside a sixty-foot yacht for a minute catching their breath. Teeth chattering, he mumbled, "We need to get inside. How are you at picking locks?"

Alex replied between her own rattling teeth, "I can improvise picks out of just about anything."

He grunted. "I was hoping you'd say that." Her mechanical genius sure was handy in a pinch. They climbed aboard the yacht and she broke off a length of wire from a taillight, fashioning it into a rough pick. It took her a while, but eventually he heard a click.

She smiled over at him and pushed open the hatch. They stepped down into a plush salon done entirely in shades of white. "Wow. Nice," she breathed.

"To heck with nice. It's out of the wind. We've got to get dry and get warm."

She poked around for a minute behind the wet bar and announced, "Water heater's turned off. No hot showers for us."

"Then we'll have to fight hypothermia the old-fashioned way—get naked and share body heat."

A rebellious look entered her gaze, but he strode down the passage to the first bedroom he came to and stepped inside. She balked in the doorway. He reverted to the tried and true, "You're not chicken, are you?"

Her gaze narrowed. She never had been able to turn down a dare, and she didn't now. She peeled off the rubber diving suit and dragged the damp T-shirt beneath over her head. He gulped at the sight of her nearly transparent bra plastered to her skin. She turned away from him to shimmy out of her jeans, and the curves of her luscious tush nearly made him groan aloud. Even covered in goose bumps, she was so sexy he could barely think straight.

He stripped off his clothes, hesitating when he reached his boxers. It wouldn't do them any good to crawl under the covers with any damp clothing on at all. It would just get the blankets wet and negate their ability to warm each other up.

Alex popped off her bra and stripped off her bikini panties so fast he barely saw them go flying. She dived under the covers, her back turned to him. He peeled off his boxers and climbed in after her.

The sheets were cold against his skin. He joined Alex in bicycling his legs vigorously and using friction to generate an immediate burst of heat. Finally, when he was breathing hard, he stopped. Better. His teeth weren't chattering anymore, and he'd warmed up from icicle to mere snow-cone status.

"Warm enough?" he murmured to the back of her head.

"Getting there."

He sighed and scooted forward, spooning his body against hers. She went board-stiff against him. "No funny business," she warned between clenched teeth.

"None." He gathered her close in his arms, doing his best to share all the heat he could with her. They lay plastered together in silence for several tense minutes. Ever so slowly, he felt a thaw between him. But whether it was more than just their body temperatures coming back up to normal, he didn't know.

As hard as it was to sleep without Alex in his arms, he was rapidly coming to the conclusion that sleeping with her in his arms was worse. How was it possible for them to be physically so close yet emotionally so far apart?

"Alex, I—" He paused, unsure of how to put any of it into words.

"What?"

"I'm sorry. I've treated you badly, and you didn't deserve any of it."

"When in particular are you referring to?"

Not going to make this easy for him, was she? "I don't know. All the way back to when Arturo died, I suppose."

She lurched. "Whoa. You want to dig up ancient history?"

"There are a lot of things I wish I could change."

She half turned in his arms to frown up at him as he propped himself on an elbow. "Look. I never blamed you for my brother's death and I still don't. He was wild. A risk taker. He was the kind of person destined to die young. You were just the unlucky soul at the wrong place and wrong time to be with him when it happened."

He'd heard the words from her before, but hearing them again did weird things to his gut. It was as if her absolution somehow piled even more guilt on top of him. Although maybe it wasn't guilt about Arty. Maybe it was guilt about her.

"I cost you your brother—" he started.

She interrupted. "He cost me that himself. He should've been sitting down and buckled in on a slippery mountain road. He knew better."

He smiled ruefully. "Not gonna let me carry that burden, are you?"

"Nope."

"Well, I'm sorry about other stuff, too."

She frowned. "Like what?"

"Like how I treated you when we were kids. I ignored you and wasn't as nice to you as I should've been."

"Oh, for crying out loud, Jim. We were kids. I was some snot-nosed brat who practically stalked you. How else were you going to treat me?"

He scowled down at her. "Why won't you let me apologize here?"

She snapped, "Because you're avoiding the real issue."

Stung, he drew back enough to really glare down at her. "Oh yeah? And what's that?"

Chapter 14

Alex's heart all but choked her. What on earth was Jim trying to do? Was he actually trying to make up with her? Did she dare let him? How did that phrase go? Fool me once, shame on him. Fool me twice, shame on me. She *knew* not to let Jim Kelley inside her guard again. He would love her and leave her without a backward glance. He'd said so himself.

"C'mon, Jim. This is about two days ago. You're sorry you jumped in the sack with me. Although why you'd wait until we're naked and in the sack again to apologize is a mystery to me."

"I am *not* sorry I jumped in the—that I made love with you!" he exclaimed.

"That's sweet of you to say. But this is me. I'm one of the guys, remember? I know the code. Be nice. Promise the girl whatever she wants, get what you want from her, and then get the hell out of Dodge."

Jim glared, seemingly at a loss for words. And then he

burst out, "Is that what you think of me? That I'd just love you and leave you?"

"Wouldn't you?"

"Hell no!" he all but shouted.

She sighed. "You don't have to lie to me to protect my feelings. I get it. You forget I've known you a very long time. I've seen how you treat your women. You might leave them a more expensive parting gift on the nightstand than most guys, but you're no different."

"And yet you'd sleep with me, thinking so poorly of me?"

The words were a sword straight through her heart. She blinked up at him rapidly, trying to clear the sudden tears pooling in her eyes and praying the light was too poor for him to spot them. "I guess so. Pathetic, huh?"

His anger dissipated as quickly as smoke in a storm. "You're not pathetic, Alex. You're actually pretty damned incredible."

She smiled up at him sadly. "I really wish you'd stop saying things like that to me."

"Why?"

"Because someday I might be tempted to believe them." She added lightly, "And then where would I be?"

He stared down at her hard as if searching for something in her eyes. She didn't know what he was looking for, but she hoped whatever it was, he wouldn't find it. He was treading dangerously close to her heart and she couldn't afford to let him hurt her any more. They still had a job to do, and they still were in mortal danger. She wasn't going to be able to hold it together if he broke down her emotional defenses any more.

He leaned down as if to kiss her. Her mind shouted at her to turn away, to run screaming from any further entanglement with this man. But her heart, ahh, her traitorous heart, it sent her arms out from under the covers. Snaking around his neck. Pulling him down to her with a sigh he'd be a fool to interpret as anything else but a welcome. God, she was an idiot!

An idiot who was suddenly dizzy and lightheaded as his lips touched hers. Her breath caught in her throat and then came fast and shallow as he deepened the kiss with a groan, half covering her body with his own and devouring her mouth and her soul.

Who was she kidding? She'd been hopelessly in love with him forever. Would be in love with him forever. Nothing he said or did was ever going to change that. And with the realization came surrender to the inevitable. A measure of peace. So be it. She was damned to love a man who would never be able to give her what she wanted.

But she was willing to take the scraps of affection he offered her. After all, scraps were better than total starvation of the soul.

He murmured, "I know better." His lips drifted across her jaw toward the base of her ear where his breath was warm and seductive. "But damned if I can stop this."

As if she ever wanted him to stop? Hah. Her chin tilted up to give him better access to her throat and her fingers toyed with the short hair at the nape of his neck.

And then he delivered the coup de grace against the sensitive column of her neck. "I've never wanted any woman the way I want you."

If only. What she wouldn't give for that to be true for more than a moment. Maybe she was an optimist—or just a fatalist—but at least they had this moment. And she didn't intend to waste it. She intended to hoard every last second of it for the long years to come.

She pulled him down to her, opening her body and her heart to him in an act of either generosity or stupidity. She didn't know which it was and, furthermore, didn't care. This was her Jim. And for today, she was his.

Maybe because she was trying to memorize every detail of their lovemaking, or maybe because she'd been on such a wild, emotional ride for the past twenty-four hours, her frantic need was replaced by a more leisurely, richer enjoyment of it all—the textures of Jim's body, the feel of his hands and mouth on hers, the way they fitted together, how they found a perfect rhythm seemingly without thought.

But what she would remember most of all was the dawning wonder in his beautiful eyes as a crescendo built between them, and then another and another, each more elegant and spectacular than the one before. And all the while he smiled at her as if that truly was his heart shining in his eyes. It was enough to make a girl half believe all his suave lies.

And then the pleasure overcame her, drawing her up and out of her body, beyond any thought at all to a place of pure sensation and raw, unfiltered feelings.

And as Jim shuddered his release, he groaned into her ear and straight into her soul, "I love you."

Her entire being froze. Absorbed the moment in awe. Something warm and foreign began to expand inside her, joy so overwhelming there was no containing it. But thankfully, her rational mind kicked in before she could go completely giddy with lovestruck insanity. Men told women they loved them all the time in the throes of sexual pleasure. It didn't mean anything. She'd overheard them talk about it at the office, for goodness sake. The consensus among the guys was that if a girl really put out, drop the L-bomb and you'd be assured of another round of great sex before the chick got wise and dumped you.

She smiled wistfully at Jim and said lightly, "I love you, too."

* * *

Jim was ecstatic to hear the words from her, but something uncomfortable buzzed in his gut. She didn't sound entirely sincere when she'd said that. Still, it made him feel like a million bucks to hear her reciprocate his feelings. He hadn't intended to tell her he loved her and certainly not at that exact moment, but now that the words were on the table between them, he was glad he'd gone ahead and gotten them out in the open. He wouldn't have guessed what a huge relief it would be to finally admit his feelings for her. It was as if a ten-ton anvil had been lifted off his chest.

And then Alex added casually, "Of course, it's not like that changes anything."

The nasty buzzing in his gut zapped him as if he'd slammed into an electric fence. "I beg your pardon?"

"Well," Alex explained, "you're still you, and I have no illusions about what that means. When this op is over, you'll move on to the next mission and the next woman. But that's okay. I've really enjoyed this…interlude."

"Interlude? I just told you I love you and you think it's an *interlude*?" Outrage boiled in his gut that she would dismiss his feelings so lightly.

"What would you call it, then?" she demanded.

"It's a goddamned life-altering event!"

"Oh, please. You probably say that to all the girls."

"I do not," he ground out. "I've never told a woman that before. You're the first and only."

She shrugged away from him as though she didn't believe him.

"It's true," he insisted. "I've never said that to anyone before you. I love you, Alex."

She frowned faintly. "Like I said. That doesn't change anything. We've still got a mission to do. Bad guys to catch. And when it's over we both have real lives to return to. This—" she paused and then rushed on "—this is an anomaly."

He leaped out of bed, too agitated to stay still. He angrily paced the tiny strip of carpet between the bed and wall. "What the hell do I have to do to convince you this is real?"

She pounced on that one without hesitation. "Walk away from this mission."

He whirled, staring in disbelief. She had to be kidding. "But I promised to catch these guys."

She spoke so reasonably it set his teeth on edge. "We're in over our heads, Jim. These Raven's Head people are too powerful for us. If you love me, put us and our safety first. Walk away from this case. Hand it over to the FBI. Then you and I—we can go away for a while. Figure out what we've got between us. Where we're going with it."

He stared at her, stunned and appalled. How in the hell was he supposed to respond to that? Finally, he managed to choke out, "If you love me, you won't ask this of me. You know how much this means to me. I vowed to my father and sister to catch her kidnappers and take them down."

"You're right. I do know how much this means to you. Your obsession with winning is bigger than your feelings for me. Hence my skepticism when you declare your love."

He threw up his hands, exasperated. "I'm capable of loving you and of wanting to see my sister's kidnappers caught and punished at the same time."

"Maybe. But here's the thing, Jim. When the right man falls in love with me, I'll be the first priority in his life. I may not have much self-respect where you're concerned. But I have enough to know that, no matter how much I love you, I won't play second fiddle to your vendetta."

And with that, she surged out of bed, gloriously naked, snatched up her clothes, and left the room, leaving him standing and staring at the closed door. She'd walked out on him?

He was the one with every right to storm out on her! She was the one being completely unreasonable. How could she ask him to abandon this mission? It was his job. Surely she didn't think he'd give up his career at the snap of her fingers. What kind of love was that for her to ask it of him?

Indignation built in his gut until it drowned the little voice at the back of his head that wondered if she might not just have a point. He was a Kelley. Love was about loyalty. Through thick and thin. Standing by your family no matter what happened. Hank might have done some stupid things in his life, but at the end of the day, his kids would forgive him and support him. It was what Kelleys did, dammit.

If Alex wanted to love him and earn his love in return, she wouldn't ask him to abandon a promise to his family. She was dead wrong. And until she realized it and admitted it, he didn't see how they had any kind of future together.

Alex sobbed into a pillow in the master bedroom. She knew she was right, but that didn't make it any easier to watch her relationship with Jim dying on the vine before it ever really got a chance to blossom and grow. It wasn't fair! But then, she'd known ever since Arturo died that life wasn't fair. Why should that change now just to suit her?

She must have cried herself to sleep because the sun was slanting through the tiny porthole when she woke up, which would make it late afternoon. The sleep might have refreshed her physically, but it had done nothing to ease the heaviness in her heart. It was a hard pill to swallow that she took second place to capturing a bunch of sleazy power mongers.

She dressed quickly, and when she stepped out into the salon, Jim was eating ravioli straight from a can and watching the television news.

"Any developments?" she asked warily. Best to keep the conversation neutral. Innocuous. She wasn't prepared to continue the argument from before. It was still too fresh and painful for her to deal with.

"They're crucifying Joe Colton. All the evidence we found and more has been leaked to the media to prove that he arranged his own fake assassination. Several key congressmen have called for impeachment hearings and are vowing to kick him out of office."

She snorted. "What do you want to bet those congressmen are in the Raven's Head Society's pockets?"

He rolled his eyes. "That's a bet I wouldn't take in a million years." He continued, "An emergency session of Congress has been called and all the candidates who are back home stumping for reelection have been recalled to Washington."

"Their campaign managers have to be loving that," she replied sarcastically.

He shrugged. "It's great theater to go after a sitting president. I'm sure they'll all find a way to turn it into votes in their precincts."

"Cynical, much?" she asked rhetorically.

He rolled his eyes. "Grow up around a politician and it's hard not to be."

She sat down across from him and picked up a tube of crackers from the coffee table in front of him. She munched on them while Jim cycled through a half-dozen versions of essentially the same story about Joe Colton's attempt to manipulate and dupe voters.

As the news moved on to other less sensational stories, Jim looked over at her grimly. "Like it or not, I don't think we've got any choice. I think we need to trick the Raven's Head Society into revealing itself."

Her heart broke a little more. He'd made his choice. Obsession over love. She replied heavily, "It won't be easy. Walter Green was right when he said they're smart."

Jim nodded. "I've been thinking. Their wallet is the place to hit them. I think that plan we talked about a while back—the one about pretending to sabotage the stock markets—might work. It's the kind of warfare they understand. If we can take them down at their strongest point, then we'll have truly defeated them."

"We'll need help," she observed warily.

He looked her in the eye for the first time and she reeled at the intensity in his electric-blue eyes. "Can you hack the international stock markets?"

She blinked. "Give me six months and I might find a back door."

He shook his head. "You've got about six hours. By now they know we stole scuba equipment from Hal and Steph's boat, which means they have a rough search radius in which to look for us. Simple math says they'll find us soon."

She loved a challenge as much as the next person, but she knew impossible when she heard it. And the stock markets were possibly the best-defended targets on the planet. The news outlets who reported stock transactions, however, were another story. "What do you have in mind once I complete this hypothetical hack?"

"I'd like to cause that panic you mentioned. Trigger institutional traders to sell all the stocks McNaught is heavily invested in like crazy."

She grinned. "They'll be forced to dump the stocks lest they lose everything. And if we're watching their computers and trading patterns, we can spot them. And then what?" she asked curiously. "What's the endgame?"

"The FBI arrests them all."

Hope flickered in her chest. "So you're willing to hand this case over to the authorities after all?"

"I'm willing to involve them at the last minute to make

arrests. We'll need the additional manpower to hit all the Raven's Head bigwigs simultaneously. But if we bring the FBI into it earlier, there'll be an information leak sure as I'm sitting here."

She had to give him that one. The Ravens undoubtedly had plants all over the Federal Bureau of Investigations. "There's still the small problem of getting into the stock-market reporting system to manipulate the trading numbers."

"You can do this, Alex. You're a genius with computers."

She laughed ruefully. "Problem is, other geniuses with computers have devised ways to keep people like me from messing with sensitive financial data like the stock markets."

"We're dead in the water without this," he said persuasively.

She frowned, thinking hard. "It would be a whole lot easier to hack into a news channel's computers than the New York Stock Exchange. And we wouldn't actually be tampering with a market, which has to be some horrible felony."

He nodded slowly. "The floor traders would know the reported numbers are wrong. The Ravens could call their brokers and find out fairly quickly that something's off."

"Unless you let the floor traders in on the scam."

He shook his head. "The Ravens will have direct plants working for them on the stock exchanges. Unless…"

She waited while he thought hard. Abruptly, a grin broke across his face. "An exercise."

"You lost me."

"What if we simulate a trading collapse? We tell the New York Stock Exchange and a few other key international markets that we're going to run a practice scenario to test the fail-safe features of the computer trading systems."

"Don't they have to announce one of those well in advance to the public so everyone knows it's an exercise?"

He shook his head. "Not if we can convince the exchange to suspend trading for a few minutes while we run the exercise. It wouldn't have to be offline for long." His voice grew more enthusiastic as he worked his way through the logic. "We ask the traders and brokers to act exactly as they would in a real panic. We tell them we'll have SEC officials posing as freaked-out investors contacting them, and they're to treat those fake investors exactly like they would in a real run on the markets."

His excitement was contagious and she added, "Then we let through the calls from the suspected Raven's Head members. They panic. Dump their stocks. Cause a real collapse in specific stocks, and lose a fortune in the process."

She and Jim traded grins. It could work. But then reality intruded. "How would we ever get the markets to cooperate with a stunt like that?"

Jim's grin widened. "Joe Colton. He's already accused of faking an assassination attempt. What's faking a stock market crash? He's toast anyway. And if this works, we catch the men who framed him and expose them. His career's saved and a bunch of greedy, power-hungry bastards go to jail."

"How on earth will you get to him to ask him to do it? You'll have to go through layers and layers of staffers, and we know at least some of them work for the Ravens."

Jim pulled out his cell phone. "Easy. I've got his personal cell phone number."

She stared. "Seriously?"

"He gave it to me when we called the White House. Said to give him a call if I needed anything from him."

"Sheesh. Must be nice to have your family's connections."

He shrugged. "It doesn't suck. A lot of blood, sweat and tears went into developing them, though, if that makes you feel better. But I don't know if all the Kelley family's connections will be enough to see this one through."

At least he'd agreed to bring in the FBI to make the arrests, and he was willing to reach out to the president for help. It was a start. Maybe not the total capitulation she'd hoped for, but a start. Now they just had to live through the next few days.

Chapter 15

Jim's first phone call was to the President of the United States. Joe Colton's deep, television-announcer voice was heard after the second ring. Without a greeting, Colton demanded, "Who is this?" The man probably wasn't fond of getting cold calls from numbers he didn't recognize on his personal phone.

Jim talked fast. He figured he had about five seconds before the man hung up on him. "This is Jim Kelley. I'm calling to offer my aid in catching the bastards who framed you for arranging the assassination attempt. I know who they are."

The belligerence of a cornered politician faded from Colton's voice, but was replaced with urgent intensity. "Thank God. What do you know?"

Jim outlined briefly the emails he and Alex had found on his father's computer, tracing them back to the president's computer, and most importantly, the confession of the shooter just before the guy blew his own brains out.

"Would you be willing to testify to all of that under oath in front of Congress?" Colton asked tightly.

"Absolutely. And so would my partner," Jim answered. Alex looked up from across the sitting room and smiled at that before burying herself in her laptop computer once more.

He continued, "My sister and her rescuer should be able to tie a few of them to organizing her kidnapping, too. And when Hank wakes up, we hope he'll be able to nail a whole bunch more of them. The Raven's Head Society has messed with my family, and we Kelleys stick together." He figured that, as a member of the tight-knit Colton clan, the president would understand what he was talking about.

"I'm listening," Colton bit out.

Jim outlined his and Alex's plan to trick the Raven's Head members into dumping specific combinations of stock and revealing themselves in so doing.

At the end of it, Colton asked, "But don't we stand a good chance of netting innocent investors who happen to hold the same combination of stocks?"

"Possible. But in the next day or so, we should have a fairly complete list of Raven's Head members. We'll watch their computers specifically for action. Any other investors we identify can be investigated and cleared or implicated later by the FBI. But in the meantime, you'll have the society's kingpins to hang out to dry in front of Congress and the almighty media."

"Pull this off, Jim, and I'll owe you for the rest of my life."

"It's about justice, sir. I'll just be happy to see these bastards behind bars."

"I don't take kindly to people attacking my reputation or framing me for some underhanded, sneaky bit of business, let alone trying to steal my job. You just tell me what you need. I want to *bury* these bastards."

"I'm glad you feel that way, sir. I'll be in touch shortly

with more specifics. In the meantime, tell *no one* about this. We have reason to believe the very highest levels of your administration are compromised by the Ravens."

"How high?" Colton asked quietly.

"Victor Metzger. Someone in your personal Secret Service detail. Security staff. I.T. staff."

A long silence greeted that announcement. Finally Colton ground out, "I want them all. Bring down the whole damn house of cards, you hear?"

"I'll do my best, sir."

Jim disconnected the call and looked over at Alex. "He's on board. We're a go."

She nodded, announcing, "I think I've got the complete stock portfolio of the McNaught Group nailed down. We mess up these thirty-four stocks and we should see Raven's Head members abandoning the sinking ship left and right. Rats ripe for the picking." Then she said reflectively, "Small problem, though. How are we going to get a complete list of Raven's Head Society members?"

He replied grimly, "How do you feel about a little visit to Chet Chandler?"

She grinned. "With the stuff we've pulled off his computer, he should sing like a canary to keep us from going public with it."

He matched her smile. "Send a canary to catch a raven."

"And how are we getting off this boat unseen so we can talk to our singing senator?"

"Alex, Alex. So little faith in my skills you have. I'm a trained Special Forces operative. I can outsmart a few thugs in suits."

Although those thugs turned out to be a pain the rear to avoid, as it turned out. He'd expected to be past them in a few minutes and it took nearly two hours of crouching in the shadows at the edge of the marina for a moment to present itself when all three of the roving Raven's Head thugs were moving away from the entry gate. He was thankful for Alex's wicked good shape as she kept up with him as they sprinted full out for the gate and slipped through it. They gained the cover of the bar across the street in the nick of time just as one of the goons returned to his post beside the gate.

"That was close," she mumbled a little shakily.

Too close. His protective instincts were surging angrily at the idea of those suits getting their filthy paws on his woman. "C'mon," he muttered. He led her through the crowded pub and into the kitchen.

A guy in front of a commercial dishwasher yelled at them that this was an employees-only area, but Jim ignored him and moved rapidly for the rear exit. He ducked outside with Alex in tow. They ran for the end of the alley and burst out onto a quaint street lined with boutiques and galleries, mostly closed now. He'd hoped to catch ol' Chet earlier in the evening, but so be it.

They walked for several blocks while he searched for a likely car to "borrow." Finally, he spotted a vintage clunker that predated fancy car-alarm systems. Using a screwdriver he'd lifted from the yacht's toolbox, he pried down the driver's-side window and unlocked the door.

He started to climb in, but Alex stopped him with a hand on his arm. "Allow me. This is my area of expertise."

Grinning, he slid across the bench seat to the passenger's side. She had the steering column disassembled so fast he could hardly believe it. He commented, "If you ever want to turn to a life of crime, you'll get rich boosting cars."

She glanced over at him and grinned as she twisted two wires together and then used needle-nosed pliers that emerged from somewhere on her person to turn the ignition assembly. The engine roared to life. "You want to drive, or shall I?"

"You know where Chandler lives. I'll watch for tails," he answered.

She eased the vehicle out of its parking space and headed for the north side of Washington and the swanky Chevy Chase address where the junior senator from Nebraska lived. Jim was relieved to see lights on in the house when they pulled into the driveway.

They walked up the front steps in tense silence. "Okay, Alex. You're on."

Alex reached out nervously to press the doorbell. In a few seconds, a female voice came out of the intercom. "It's very late. The senator will take interviews in the morning during his regular office hours."

"Hi, Mrs. Chandler. This is Alex Mendez. I'm sorry to disturb you at home so late. I have something urgent to show the senator."

"You?" the woman exclaimed. "I heard you were in some trouble…"

Alex glanced over at Jim in alarm. Apparently, the Raven's Head Society had been at work destroying her reputation and credibility in the event she and Jim tried to do something exactly like this and approach the senator directly. He nodded encouragingly.

She spoke into the intercom. "Some false rumors have been circulated about me by people frantic to prevent me from revealing something I discovered a few days ago. That's why I'm here, in fact. To show the senator."

"I'll get Chet."

They stood under the uncomfortable glare of the porch lights for several long minutes before Chet Chandler opened the front door, a patently false smile pasted on his face. "Alex! And your friend from the McNaught fundraiser. Jim, isn't it?"

"That's right, sir. Can we step into your office for a moment? I have something to show you. Believe me, you're going to want to see it."

"Of course." The senator glanced briefly over her shoulder into the night and Jim tensed beside her. Alex swore mentally. Before he'd answered the door, Chet had called someone from the Raven's Head Society. He was looking out there to see if his backup had arrived yet. She and Jim didn't have much time.

Jim closed the study door quietly as Chandler moved around behind his desk and sat down in a position of power. Nice try, but it wasn't going to help him.

Vividly aware of the Raven's Head goons en route, she said, "Let me cut right to the chase, Senator Chandler. I work for the U.S. government and was placed in your office to monitor your activities. It has come to our attention that you work for a group called the Raven's Head Society."

"I categorically deny working for anybody but my constituents in the fine state of Nebraska—"

"Cut the crap," Jim interrupted. "We've got proof, and lots of it. Alex has been monitoring and recording all of your computer activity for some time. We've got emails, records of campaign contributions, video of my sister being held captive by your employers, the works. You're going down in flames, Chandler."

The man blanched and spluttered, speechless.

Alex, who'd been designated good cop for this encounter dived in. "There is, however, a way you can save yourself and your political career. Give us names, Chet. We've got most of them already, of course. But fill in the gaps for us. Tell us who we've missed and we'll destroy everything we've collected on you."

"How can I believe you? You've made copies and you'll just keep on blackmailing me. No. I won't do it."

Jim intervened silkily. He made a menacing bad cop. "Then let me put it to you this way, Chet. We know enough of the names to make a severe dent in the Raven's Head Society without your help. When the survivors find out you let a government agent not only work for you but have free access to your personal computer and all your files and correspondence, they're naturally going to assume you're the source of our list of Raven's Head members. And they'll kill you for revealing their identities. You're a dead man."

Alex followed Jim's lead and let the senator ponder that one for a few seconds.

Then she spoke gently. "It's over, Senator Chandler. The only way to save yourself is to help us. We've been authorized to grant you full immunity from prosecution if you'll give us a complete listing of Ravens."

"But I don't know them all," Chandler said desperately. "You have to understand, they're very secretive. They compartmentalize their organization so no one knows who everyone is. I could give you who I know, but it would be far from everyone."

Jim leaned forward aggressively. "What makes you think you're the first or only person who's talking to us? You're not even remotely the most important person we're talking to. We're only approaching you at all as a courtesy to Alex. Seems she liked you and wanted to cut you a break."

The senator looked at her gratefully. "I'll do what I can," he said heavily. He pulled out a pad of paper and started writing rapidly. He scribbled for several minutes without interruption. He read through the list, added a few more names, and then tore off the sheet.

"You might as well pass us the entire pad," Jim commented blandly. "That way the Raven's Head goons on their way here won't find it, read the impression of the list you made, and shoot you on the spot."

Chandler lurched and shoved the whole legal pad and list across the desk.

"And speaking of Raven goons, we're going to need to borrow your wife's car, Chet," Jim said casually.

"Hey now—"

"I can call the FBI right now and have them issue a warrant for your arrest," Jim said smoothly.

"The key's in the kitchen," Chet said, surly.

Alex piped up. "We'll return it to you as soon as we can."

They stood up to leave and Jim added, "Your best bet is to tell the guys about to get here that you gave us nothing and stick to that story at all costs. You don't strike me as the type to hold out for long if they decide to torture you to find out exactly what you told us."

As Chet blanched yet again, Alex raced after Jim. He must've heard the car pull up quietly out front, too. They snagged the key fob for Mrs. Chandler's Mercedes and burst into the garage.

"We'll never get past them unseen," Alex panted as she leaped into the passenger seat.

"Nope. It's gonna be a balls-to-the-wall chase."

He started the car and glanced over as she latched her seat belt. Their eyes met briefly.

She murmured, "I'm not Arturo. You won't let me get hurt."

And with that reassurance ringing in his ears, he opened the garage door and floored the accelerator.

Car chases weren't nearly as glamorous in reality as television made them out to be. They were violent, teeth-jarring, neck-wrenching affairs, and this one made Alex feel like fruit in a blender. It quickly became obvious that both cars were evenly matched in speed and cornering ability, and whoever was driving the late-model sedan behind them was about as skilled a driver as Jim. It was going to boil down to who was more willing to die, the chasers or the chasees.

Of course, the other bit the television failed to portray was how rapidly the local police got involved in a high-speed chase.

"Call Kittredge," Jim gritted out as he swerved between two slower cars and ran a red light. "Get the cops off us."

She made the call, but had an inspiration. "Austin, it's Alex. Can you call the Metro police and explain to them who we are? We've got Raven's Head Society thugs on our tail and we need to get rid of them."

"What are you two up to?" Jim's boss exclaimed.

"We'll explain later. Right now we need your help."

"Sure. Let me get to the other phone."

It took no more than two minutes for the orders to pass through the Washington Metro Police chain of command and back to Kittredge who relayed, "Turn right onto Wisconsin Avenue when you get there. A police barricade will be set up but left open for you two. Once your vehicle passes through it, they'll throw down the spikes and roll concrete barricades into the street. Got it?"

"Got it. Thanks, Austin."

"You'll call me when you're in the clear?"

"You've got it." She hung up as Jim careened around the corner onto Wisconsin. Only seconds later the squealing tires of their pursuers screeched behind them. A Christmas-bright display of flashing lights blossomed before them. It was going to be a close call for them to get through the police line in time for the barricade to go up behind them.

"Here goes nothing," Jim muttered. He floored the accelerator and the Mercedes's powerful engine roared forward. Thankfully, German cars were built to cruise the Autobahn at speeds well in excess of a hundred miles per hour. The vehicle bounded through the phalanx of police cars and vans.

Alex turned in her seat to watch as the police leaped into action behind them.

Four loud bangs announced the explosive deflation of their pursuers' tires, and then a mighty crash of noise announced the other car's impact with a concrete crash barricade.

Jim's foot lifted off the accelerator and the car slowed rapidly. He muttered, "Remind me to thank the chief of police the next time I talk to him."

They drove sedately away from the mess behind them. She had no idea where Jim was going, and neither, she suspected, did he.

When her adrenaline had come back down to something approaching human, her brain engaged once more. Reluctantly, she said, "You do realize Chandler's right, don't you? We have no way of knowing if we've got the entire list of Raven's Head members."

He sighed. "Yes, I do. And I know what I have to do."

He said no more, but guided the vehicle with clear purpose toward some destination.

She was startled when they pulled up in front of Walter Reed Army Hospital. "What are we doing here?"

"Getting the rest of that list, I hope."

She frowned and followed him inside. He led her quickly to the ICU and they stepped into its sterile brilliance.

"I'm sorry, sir," a nurse said officiously. "Visiting hours are over."

"I'm aware of that, ma'am," Jim said politely. "I need to speak to the attending physician on the floor right away."

"And you are?"

"Jim Kelley. Hank Kelley's son. Please hurry, ma'am. This is an emergency."

Apparently, that word carried a lot of clout around here, for in moments a tall man in a doctor's white lab coat strode out to the nurses' station. "What's this about Senator Kelley?

Your father is improving slowly and we are hopeful he'll make a full recovery."

"Unfortunately, I can't wait that long. I need you to wake him up now."

The doctor lurched. "I can't do that."

"Sure you can. You stop giving him the meds that are knocking him out."

"It would be incredibly dangerous. The swelling is less, but it is by no means gone."

Jim sighed. "This is a matter of national security. And if you'll check your records, you'll see that my mother gave me full power of attorney over my father while he's in here. I believe I have the legal right to insist that you cease inducing coma."

"This is highly irregular and I'm not about to let some panicked family member dictate how I care for my patient—" the doctor started.

Jim waved the man to silence. "Save me the indignant speech. I get it. I'd react the same way if I were in your shoes. But here's the thing. This truly is a matter of national security, and it's classified enough that I can't tell you anything about it. But my father must be woken up *now*. What I need you to do is to figure out how to do that as safely as possible. I only need him alert for a few minutes and then you can knock him out for as long as your heart desires."

"I cannot do that, Mr. Kelley. Nurse, call security—"

"Belay that order," Jim bit out. "I'm going to make a phone call, and I want you to talk to the person on the other end. If you still refuse to wake up my father, my associate and I will leave the hospital immediately. Is that a deal?"

The doctor frowned, clearly highly irritated by the entire situation. Jim reminded himself to compliment the man on his commitment to his patient's best interests after this was all over.

As he pulled out his cell phone to wake up the president, Alex murmured in concern, "Are you sure about this? You heard the doctor. This could *kill* your father."

As if he needed that little reminder. His gut was already twisted so tight he could hardly breathe. He replied shortly, "You said it yourself. We have to have the entire list for this to work."

"But, Jim. It's *Hank*."

"I'm well aware of that," he snapped. "You tell me what he would want. If he knew risking his life would bring down the whole network of people who kidnapped his daughter and nearly killed him, what would Hank want?"

She asked reasonably, "Is this about what he would want or what *you* want? Are you letting your obsession cloud your better judgment here?"

She could really let go of the whole obsession argument. His voice rose slightly. "I'm trying to stop a group of madmen who want to rule the world through the Oval Office. How is that wrong?"

She subsided unhappily, watching glumly as Jim finished dialing the president's cell phone.

"Jim?" The president didn't sound as if he'd been sleeping.

"I'm sorry to bother you, sir. I need you to speak to a doctor who's with me. He's refusing to wake up my father. I need Hank to tell me who all's in the Raven's Head Society before we spring our little trap."

"Chandler was a bust?" Colton asked grimly.

"Oh, no. He coughed up a list. But he also confirmed our fear that the Society works in separate cells for security purposes."

"Is it time for me to lean on Victor, then?"

"I'm afraid so, sir. And remember what we talked about. Once he learns that you're aware of who he works for, he can't be allowed to speak to *anyone*. No guards. No staff. No one. He's got to be completely isolated."

"Victor won't get a message to his handlers. You have my word on it as a Colton."

"That's good enough for me, sir. Here's the doctor."

Jim passed the phone to the physician. The poor man listened for a few moments in silence and then stammered, "Of course…I understand…best possible care afterward… yes, sir." He handed the phone back to Jim. The guy looked a little pale around the gills.

"Satisfied?" Jim asked grimly.

The doctor cleared his throat. "It'll take about two hours for the effect of the medications to wear off. Do you want any other family members present in case he doesn't survive this?"

The nurse squawked in disbelief, and the physician threw her a quelling look. "Believe me, Karen, when the man says it's a matter of national security, he's not kidding."

The next two hours passed at a snail's pace. Jim felt like a heel for risking his father's life like this, and it didn't help that every glance Alex threw at him was filled with reproach. Finally he muttered from beside Hank's bed, "What choice do I have? We need to know what he knows."

"You could let other people do this. They could lean on your father's staff. Get names from them. We could search his office files and computers. Maybe we'd find something."

He retorted, "If the Raven's Head Society cleaned out his home office, what makes you think they didn't already clean out his Congressional office?"

Her shoulder rose in a sigh. "I just hate to see you endanger Hank."

"You think I *like* doing this?" He couldn't keep a raw note of anguish out of his voice.

She came around the bed and wrapped her arms around his waist. "I'm sorry. I know this is hard for you."

He hung on to her tightly, stunned at how much he needed her comfort—and how much comfort he drew from her presence. Since when had she become his emotional rock? He'd always been the strong one, the older brother, the protector. He must be closer to the ragged edge of losing it than he'd realized.

They stood like that for a long time, just holding one another. She healed him as no other person could. How was it she always made things better for him? She was the one person he could always count on being there for him no matter what he did. Hell, even when he'd had a part in killing her brother, she'd been there for him.

"He's starting to wake up," the doctor announced. "I'm going to try to bring him up just enough to talk to you, and then I want to put him back under. You'll only have a few minutes. Understand?"

"That's all I need," Jim said grimly. He leaned down over the bed, taking his father's dry hand in his, tubes and all. "Hey, Pop."

Hank Kelley's eyes drifted open, unfocused.

The doctor murmured, "Give him another minute or two."

Jim waited patiently. And then, simultaneously, his father's gaze seemed to clear and Hank squeezed Jim's hand.

"Welcome back," Jim murmured. "Sorry to wake you, but we're closing in on the guys who shot you and kidnapped Lana, and I need your help. Do you understand me?"

A strong squeeze was his answer to that.

"I'm going to read you a list of names. We know these people are members of the Raven's Head Society." Hank's hand jerked at the mention of the society. "I need you to tell me if we missed anyone and, if so, who. We're going to nail them all tomorrow, but we need to make sure none of them get away. Okay?"

Hank nodded infinitesimally.

The doctor murmured, "Don't move your head, Senator. You're still very fragile."

Jim took the list Chandler had written and the one Alex had printed earlier. He held both sheets in front of Hank's eyes. His father studied the list carefully as Jim read it aloud to him.

"Are there more names we should add?" Jim finally asked.

Hank rasped in a parched, hoarse whisper. "Yes."

Jim spent the next few minutes bending down uncomfortably with his ear in front of his father's mouth to catch every name Hank recited. Jim conveyed them to Alex, who added them to the list. And he had to admit, a few of the names his father whispered shocked the hell out of him. It was hard to believe how deep into the American academic, economic, business and political establishments the Ravens had sunk their claws.

"That's enough, Mr. Kelley," the doctor murmured. "Time to wrap things up."

"Can you think of any more names before the doctor puts you back to sleep?" Jim asked his father.

Hank squeezed his hand one more time. Jim leaned down close to catch the final name.

Hank whispered achingly, "Love…you. And your brothers and Lana."

Jim took a ragged breath while Hank gathered his strength one last time. He barely breathed, "And Sarah. Tell your mother…I always…loved her…in spite of it all…."

Jim's throat tightened and his eyes felt inexplicably hot and wet all of a sudden. Hank might have been a born-again bastard over the years, but at the end of the day, the man's last thoughts were of his children. His wife. And love.

Jim forced words past the horrible burning, choking sensation in his throat. "I'll tell them. I promise. But you do what the doctor says and get better, okay? Then you can tell them yourself."

Hank squeezed his hand one last time, so weakly that Jim barely felt it. Dear God. His father was slipping away before his very eyes. They were losing Hank.

The doctor started the IV drip, and as Hank's eyes drifted closed, Jim reached out to gently brush a lock of hair off his father's forehead. He murmured thickly, "I love you, too, Pop. Sweet dreams."

Alex's hand slipped into his, offering him silent comfort. He wrapped an arm around her shoulder and looked up at the physician bleakly. "Take care of him, Doc. Please don't make me responsible for killing my father, too."

The physician nodded. "We'll do our best. And good luck. It sounds like you're going to need it."

Alex's heart ached for Jim. She didn't think she could've made the same decision in the same situation. Her dad was all she had in the world. Could she risk him for the sake of the greater good? She didn't think she was that courageous.

As they headed out of the hospital, she sighed. Was she being too hard on Jim to insist he give up this mission for her? His family was everything to him. She got that—she'd grown up among the Kelleys and seen their fierce loyalty to each other up close and personal. They played hard and fought hard and loved hard.

Thing was, she just couldn't face the future if something happened to Jim. He might be diving headfirst into a suicide mission, and the hell of it was she had no choice but to go with him. She might not be a Kelley, but she loved him as hard as any Kelley.

Jim guided the car out of the parking lot. "Joe Colton's

going to call me as soon as he forces names from Victor Metzger. That should give us a pretty complete idea of who to have the FBI monitor when the sting goes down."

"And you're sure the judge issuing the warrants won't squeal?"

"Austin Kittredge is going to take him into protective custody just to make sure. The judge will be pissed, but once he realizes the scope of this conspiracy, he'll get over it."

She nodded. "I have a few last-minute preparations to make. If you'll drop me off at the love nest, you can head on over to the FBI to coordinate getting all the surveillance in place. I'll be ready to go when you give me the thumbs-up."

She hated this last part of the plan where they split up, but she had no choice. There was one tiny detail she'd omitted telling Jim. Okay, one huge detail.

It was the part where the Raven's Head's Society's own computer geniuses were going to track down her location. They'd know exactly where to find her long before the sting was all said and done. She was going to be a sitting duck.

But it was the only way. Jim had suggested she run the operation from FBI headquarters or maybe their unit offices, and she'd vetoed the idea. The Raven's Head Society's hackers would peg the source of the hack as a government computer and know the sting for the setup it was instantly.

She had to do it old-school. It had to be from her own laptop on a private server. No cover. No protection. Just her and the Ravens.

If Jim knew the Raven's computer geeks could find her, he would want to surround her with a dozen FBI agents, all hovering vulturelike with guns and grim stares. There were two problems with that: one, she couldn't work with a roomful of people staring at her. Two, and more importantly, the Raven's Head hit team would come in with guns blazing and mow down whoever stood in their path to her. She couldn't have the lives of a bunch of FBI agents on her conscience.

If she was alone, she could move faster. Respond more nimbly to get out of the way. Her best bet was to make as small a target of herself as she could. To be a mouse. Heck, to be a flea on a mouse. And most importantly of all, she needed Jim to be safe. No way would she be able to do the job and then survive afterward if she was spending all her mental energy being terrified for his safety.

It didn't take being an experienced field operative to know that she and Jim, or she and Jim and a team of FBI agents, couldn't win against a crack team of the Ravens' hit men. When a killer was willing to die to get his job done, such an assassin was darned near impossible to stop. Jim's unit preached about the dangers of suicide killers all the time.

Her only option was to make sure Jim, or anyone else who might try to protect her, was well clear of the bloodbath and survived the day.

Seeing him and Hank together had only strengthened her resolve to not tell Jim. His family needed him. She could hardly stand to think about her pop losing his only remaining child, but if the worst happened and she failed, the Kelleys would rally around Rikki Mendez.

She couldn't go on without Jim. It might be lame, but it was the God's honest truth: better her than him if one of them ended up dying on this op.

Pulling into the underground parking garage, she parked beside the Beast and gave it an affectionate pat as she passed by. It would go back to her father if anything happened to her. She hoped he'd enjoy it. Picturing him cruising the Rockies with the top down and his head thrown back to the blue sky made her tear up for a second.

She wasn't going to die, darn it! This would turn out all

right. The good guys would win the day, and both she and Jim would be fine. Any other outcome was unthinkable.

Taking a shaky breath, she hoisted the bag of computer equipment the FBI had loaned her—exact duplicates of her laptop and the one she'd used to set up the shadow of Chet Chandler's computer. It hadn't even been a week since she'd done that, but it seemed like a lifetime ago.

She let herself into the love nest and immediately disabled both of the bugs. That alone might be enough to trigger a Raven's Head squad to come investigate. But if they picked up the sounds of her working on her computers, they'd come for sure. She swept the place for any more electronic surveillance devices but found none. After she and Jim had fled the place, the Ravens apparently hadn't felt it necessary to supplement the surveillance in here. Their mistake.

She set up her computers rapidly and loaded the fake stock-market-crash program into both. The SEC had provided it to her. She supposed she shouldn't have been surprised that the Security Exchange Commission—the policing body of publicly traded stock exchanges—had several such scenarios built and sitting around in their safes waiting to be run sometime.

What had really surprised her, however, was how enthusiastic the select rank-and-file floor traders they'd been forced to bring into the operation had been to participate in a sting of corporate high rollers. Particularly those responsible for profiteering from subtle stock-market manipulation.

The floor traders had agreed to look out for any hint of brokers figuring out the scam before it had been allowed to run its course and to head off or shout down those individuals if necessary.

All she had left to do now was wait. That was the worst part. It gave her plenty of time to replay her past few days with Jim. To remember the highs and lows, the laughter and arguments. And the loving. Above all, the loving. She remembered the sound of the words *I love you* coming from Jim's lips. He might not have meant them, but she'd gotten to hear them once. And that was more than she'd ever hoped for.

Finally, her phone vibrated. Jim. She put the device to her ear. "Whenever you're ready," he said. "We've got everyone on the list under electronic surveillance."

She turned on the television to a financial-news network. Might as well enjoy the show in living color. "Here goes, then. And, Jim?"

"Yes?"

"Whatever happens, it's been a great ride. Thanks."

"Uh, yeah. Sure." He sounded confused. But he'd understand soon enough. If the Raven's Head killers turned out to be faster and smarter than her, he'd definitely understand later what she'd meant.

She hit the send button.

Chapter 16

The operations center at FBI headquarters was quieter than he expected it would be, but then things hadn't really hit the fan yet, either. It had turned out to be ridiculously easy to simulate a micro crash in the stock market. Alex's computer would feed in a few strategic false trades of the targeted stocks at sharply lower prices, and the sudden drop in share price would trigger a wave of automatic institutional sell-offs of the stock in question, called stop-loss programs.

The cascade of automatic sales would drive the stock price even lower, triggering option sales known as puts which, in turn, would drive the price even lower still. After-hours brokerages overseas would catch wind of the problem, triggering their own frantic sell-off of the targeted stocks.

And last but not least, the scattered stockbrokers of private investors all over the country would roll in on the action, wildly dumping stock as fast as they could in a panicked effort to recover at least a little value for their mom-and-pop investors. In a matter of minutes all thirty-four of the Mc-Naught-held stocks would be in simulated free fall. In point of fact, real trading on all the stocks would secretly be halted.

And in the meantime, wiretaps and internet surveillance of all the suspected Raven's Head/McNaught members would be waiting to record the specific combination of stock sales that only Raven's Head members should make.

"We are in play," someone called across the ops center. "Look sharp, everybody."

Jim watched impatiently as rows of computer security experts huddled over their monitors, absorbing a mind-numbing flow of information, sifting through it for what they sought.

The stock prices began to fall. They plummeted rapidly and only picked up speed as they went. It was a breathtaking display of just how fragile the stock markets could be. He made a mental note to divest some of his holdings into less volatile investments once this mess was all over.

The first tech called out, "I've got one. Ernie Bradshaw."

It figured he'd be the first rat to jump the sinking ship.

More names got called out. An FBI agent beside Jim ticked the names off on a clipboard as the surveillance specialists spotted incriminating trades. And then other names started rolling in. Names not on the list. Rich, powerful people from every walk of life. They would be taken into custody, too, and questioned at length about their possible involvement with the Ravens and McNaught.

The first financial news channel made a breaking news story and the techs started calling out names thick and fast after that. After another ten minutes or so, the stock dumping began to wind down. They'd probably bagged all the fish they were going to.

"Cue the president," Jim ordered quietly.

The agent-in-charge spoke into a cell phone to a corresponding agent located beside Joe Colton in the private train station beneath the Capitol Building.

A few minutes later, a closed-circuit monitor on the wall showed the president walking down the center aisle of the House of Representatives, interrupting the joint session of Congress convened to discuss his impeachment. A buzz of consternation went up on the House floor as his tall form was spied striding down the aisle.

The press would go crazy, assuming Colton was there to resign. Jim grinned. They were in for a hell of a shock.

The camera panned over the members of Congress where the sharks could be seen circling gleefully—some grinning openly and passing each other thumbs-up in the crowd. That footage should prove interesting to analyze after this fiasco was concluded. But first, there was the delicate matter of timing to attend to.

"Tell your field agents to stand by," Jim told the agent beside him.

The man nodded tersely and relayed the order to dozens of field agents in place near the various Raven's Head suspected members.

"They'll go on the president's orders and not before," Jim reminded everyone.

The room went mostly quiet as President Colton prepared to speak. All the major news channels cut into their regular programming to cover the president's statement.

But then into the silence, one of the techs called out, "I've got traffic on one of the computer servers we're monitoring. An encrypted message. It's…" A pause while the decryption program did its magic. "It's a kill order to an apparent hit squad."

"Who's the target?" the agent-in-charge called back.

"Some guy named Alex Mendez."

Jim jolted as though he'd been hit with a cattle prod. "Who sent it?"

"It originated from somebody called Roscoe Harrington."

The man in charge of wet ops for the Raven's Head Society.

"That's a legitimate threat," Jim shouted as he sprinted for the door. He called out the address of the love nest as he dashed out of the room and ran for his car. The apartment was only a dozen blocks away. He had to get there before Roscoe's team of killers. He *had* to.

He drove like a madman. He had faith that FBI agents were on their way behind him, but they didn't understand. This was Alex. He couldn't lose her! Not after he'd just found her. Their life together was barely beginning, dammit.

The drive took only a few minutes, but a few lifetimes passed in his mind's eye. Bouncing on the bed with her and laughing their heads off. Dissing her car. Dancing with her in a red dress that stole his breath away. And making love to her…

If he could've pushed the gas pedal through the floor, he would have. He dialed his phone one-handed and nearly crashed into a parked car in so doing, but he managed to punch out her number.

He listened in horror as her phone rang and rang. She should've picked it up immediately. Something was terribly wrong. *Get out, Alex! Run, baby!* He mentally shouted warnings at her, even knowing they were useless. He did curse out loud, pounding his fists on the steering wheel. He threw his car around the last corner. As he screeched into the parking garage, he drove right up to the stairwell door and leaped out, running before his feet touched the ground.

The door was charred and hanging, bent and broken from hinges half torn out of the wall.

Alex's laughing face danced in his mind's eye. Her eyes

were big and dark, sparkling expectantly as she waited for him to catch the joke.

Be alive. Just be alive, he begged her as he tore up the stairs.

He reached the third-floor door. It was jimmied open but not blown to bits. They'd tried to sneak up here, then. He pulled his sidearm and moved forward cautiously into the hallway. A distant wail of sirens became audible. The FBI and police, no doubt. But they wouldn't be in time. Whatever was going to happen would be over in the next few seconds.

The love nest's door was closed. It was all he could do not to burst in, guns blazing, but every ounce of training he'd ever had warned him that would get Alex killed faster than anything else he could do. He had to know what was on the other side of that door first.

He pressed his ear to the panel. He heard a juicy sound and then a grunt of pain from the far side of the room. Over by the computer desk, he estimated.

Another thud and a groan—this time distinctly female. The bastards were beating her up? Probably trying to extract information from her before they killed her. He did see red, then. They were *hurting* her? Then they would *die.*

He fell into a cold state of killing rage as he slid his key card into the hotel-style lock. The green light flashed. He turned the knob and leaped through the door all in one blindingly fast movement.

He took in the scene in an instant. Two men. One with weapons trained on Alex. The second standing over her, where she sat tied in a chair. Jim double-tapped a pair of bullets into the chest of the first man as the second one turned and reached for his gun.

Alex heaved violently behind the second attacker and flung herself and her chair into the back of the guy's legs. As his gun cleared his jacket, the thug staggered. That was all the opening Jim needed. He took aim and shot the guy directly in the heart.

Her would-be killers never had a chance. That was his woman and no one was taking her from him. He raced around the end of the sofa, keeping his gun trained on the downed men. Neither moved.

Alex's eyelids were split and nearly swollen shut, but those eyes of hers were as expressive as ever. And right now they reflected a terror he sincerely hoped never to see in them again as long as he lived.

"Are you all right?" he rasped.

She nodded and choked back a sob.

He knelt to check each of her assailants. They were both dead. Gently he righted her, chair and all. He cut the duct tape they'd used to restrain her but didn't pull it off her skin. "Let me get some nail-polish remover and we'll get that tape off you."

He knew from his own training that it hurt like a bitch to yank duct tape off of human skin. They went into the bathroom together and spent the next minutes dousing her wrists in the acetone-based solvent.

He wedged a fingernail under a corner of the tape and then smiled down at her ruefully. "Ready?"

She nodded and braced herself.

"Last time I ever hurt you, honey, I swear." And then he ripped the tape off.

She hissed and her forearms bloomed rectangles of angry red. He gently pressed a cold washcloth to them. "The sting will pass in a minute," he promised.

She shoved aside the cloth. "To heck with that," she announced, launching herself at him. He caught her against him, laughing…and something else…something that made his breath come in uneven gasps and his face wet. Or maybe that was her face that was wet and rubbing up against his. Or maybe he didn't care. She was *alive*.

"God almighty, I thought I'd lost you," he said brokenly against her mouth between kisses without number. "Why didn't you tell me they'd be able to trace you?"

"You'd have insisted on putting me somewhere with fancy security and the Raven's Head hackers would've known it was a trap. This was the only way."

"You courageous idiot," he half laughed, half lectured. "Don't you understand that I can't lose you? Ever?"

She pulled back far enough to stare up at him, a million questions swimming in her eyes.

"Freeze! Lay down your weapon!"

Jim complied readily with the SWAT officer's command. He released Alex and locked his fingers behind his head while the man secured the scene. In moments, though, the cop announced from the doorway, "All clear. You may, uh, resume what you were doing."

"And what exactly were we doing?" Alex asked as she stepped into his arms once more.

"I believe I was proposing to you."

She went utterly still. Stared. "Come again?"

"Will you marry me, Alex? Make me the happiest man in the world. I want to spend the rest of my life with you. And please don't ever make me worry that I'm going to lose you again like that. My heart couldn't take it a second time."

"Well, all right, then. If your heart can't take any more shocks, I guess I have no choice," she replied dryly.

In an agony of suspense, he blurted, "Is that a yes?"

"Yes, it's a yes, smarty pants."

He swept her off her feet and whirled her around in a circle of pure joy. Her laughter rose to mingle with his. "Where have you been my whole life?" he demanded.

"Right in front of you, Jim. I was right here all the time."

He felt like a blind man who'd been given the gift of sight. Finally, he'd come out of the long darkness of his life alone and into the light of Alex's love.

"You were right about one thing and wrong about one other," he said when they finally stopped spinning and clung to one another dizzily.

"How's that?"

"You were right that it's been a great ride. But you were entirely wrong about it being over. The ride's just beginning, baby."

Chapter 17

Alex looked around the backyard at the Kelley clan, family and friends, both old and new, assembled at the Kelley ranch in Maple Cove, Montana. It hadn't been long since they'd all been together like this—Dylan and Cindy's wedding last month had brought most of them back for a reunion. The newlyweds were back from their honeymoon and currently making goo-goo faces in the porch swing at their infant son.

Alex leaned down affectionately to the silver-haired man in the wheelchair beside her. "Can I get you anything, Hank?"

"A bunch of grandchildren would be nice."

She laughed. "How about you let Jim and me get married first? And besides, it looks like Lana's just about to give you your second grandbaby." She glanced over at her future sister-in-law's gigantic belly. The poor girl looked about ready to burst, but she also looked positively radiant relaxing in Deacon's arms. "Is it true she's having a girl?"

"So I hear." Hank shook his head sagely. "A whole lot more

trouble than boys to raise, but they love you sweeter, those girls."

Alex laughed. "Well, you're about to have a bunch of daughters-in-law. Do we count?"

He patted her hand. "Absolutely. As long as you girls get cracking and give me the next generation of Kelleys without delay. I want a whole slew of grandkids."

Alex grinned. "Count me and Jim in. We both love big families. Looks like some of the others are going to be up for it, too." She gazed around at the gathering of family. *Her* family.

Cole Kelley was lounging with his fiancée, Bethany. They were up next in this year's hit parade of Kelley weddings. They got dibs on a Christmas wedding because they needed to squeeze it in between her dad's broken leg healing enough to walk Bethany down the aisle and calving season on the ranch.

Alex gazed down fondly at the stunning diamond engagement ring on her own finger. She and Jim had agreed to wait until next summer to tie the knot officially just to give the family a break from continuous trips back to Montana to celebrate births and weddings. But she'd already moved into Jim's townhouse and transferred to a technology development unit at Fort Belvoir so there would be no issues regarding her being engaged to her boss.

Even the Kelley family friends seemed to be getting into the marriage act. Lana's BFF, Caitlin O'Donahue and her fiancé, Rhett, were in town to plan their wedding. Alex's gaze roamed across the crowd, and she spotted them talking with Caitlin's father, Mickey, who'd been cleared of all wrongdoing regarding the Raven's Head Society. In fact, he had supposedly shared valuable information with the FBI that was helping build its case against the blessedly defunct secret society.

"Can I get you something to eat or drink, sir?" Gage Prescott asked Hank from behind Alex. For a big man, Hank's long-time bodyguard, Gage, moved really quietly. She hadn't heard him approach at all.

"No, but you can let me flirt with that beautiful lady on your arm," Hank retorted.

Gage's fiancée, Kate Rogers, blushed beside him.

"How's your sister, Katie?" Hank asked.

"Better. Living in Seattle. Her ex is in jail and she's finally getting on with her life."

Hank looked around the gathering. "Looks like a lot of us Kelleys are doing that. Must be something in the water."

Gage and Kate laughed and drifted off.

Just then, Alex spied a familiar figure stepping out of the kitchen hesitantly. *That* was the last person she'd expected to see here today! She murmured, "Uh, I think you've got a visitor, Hank."

The senator looked up sharply and spotted his estranged wife on the porch. He muttered, "Well, hell."

Alex started to move away but Hank grabbed her hand more strongly than any legitimate convalescent possibly could. She *knew* it. He *was* faking the whole too weak to walk thing to get sympathy from his family.

"Don't you abandon me, girlie. You're family now. We Kelleys stick together."

"I'd heard that," she commented dryly.

"Hello, Hank."

"Sarah. You're looking good."

"Thank you. So are you. It seems the reports of your impending demise were somewhat exaggerated."

He grinned. "Kelleys are hard to keep down."

The two of them stared at each other long enough for Alex to get good and uncomfortable. If only the old man would let go of her hand, she'd sneak away. But as it was, he had a death grip on it that was nuking the circulation in her fingers. Hank and Sarah had a whole lot of history together, and she had a feeling a good chunk of it had just replayed silently between the two of them.

"I came to give you these." Sarah handed a sheaf of official-looking papers to Hank.

He didn't glance down at them. "You're going through with it, then?" he said soberly.

"No, Hank. That's the court order dismissing my divorce petition. I thought you might like a copy."

Hank burst up out of the wheelchair and swept his wife into his arms. "Sarah Mistler Kelley, you've just made me the happiest man alive!" he bellowed.

The party came to an abrupt and complete halt. Alex wondered wryly if folks were more shocked to see Hank standing or to see him kissing his wife like there was no audience and no tomorrow.

"What's this?" Dylan asked cautiously.

"It appears your mother has decided to forgive me," Hank announced happily.

"I'm not sure about that," Sarah corrected. "But I am willing to give us another chance."

"That's good enough for me, darlin'. I can work with that." Hank beamed.

Jim came over to Alex's side to offer his parents his congratulations. Alex snuggled against his side, reveling in his easy strength. In a few moments, they'd all gathered around—Dylan and Cindy, Gage and Kate, Cole and Bethany, Rhett and Caitlin, Deacon and Lana.

Hank held up a glass of wine someone had passed him. "I think a toast is in order. Here's to all of us. To family. To laughter. To love that overcomes all obstacles. And to grandchildren. Lots and lots of grandchildren!"

Glasses clinked, warm glances and smiles were traded,

and silent promises exchanged by all to fulfill the last part of that toast sooner rather than later. The Kelley clan was about to grow. A lot.

* * * * *

A sneaky peek at next month...

INTRIGUE...

BREATHTAKING ROMANTIC SUSPENSE

My wish list for next month's titles...

In stores from 21st December 2012:

☐ Grayson – Delores Fossen

& Dade – Delores Fossen

☐ Breathless Encounter – Cindy Dees

& Switched – HelenKay Dimon

☐ Cavanaugh's Surrender – Marie Ferrarella

& Montana Midwife – Cassie Miles

☐ Colton Destiny – Justine Davis

Available at WHSmith, Tesco, Asda, Eason, Amazon and Apple

Just can't wait?

1212/46

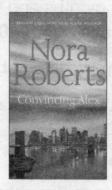